Gerald Killingworth is a playwright with numerous productions on the London 'fringe'. After reading English at Cambridge, he became a teacher, spending some years at schools in Greece before returning to Britain. He is now the Head of English at a school in Surrey. He has written several novels for adults and children, but this is his first to be published. He also enjoys British folklore and folk singing and is the Secretary of the Greensleeves Morris Men who are based in Wimbledon where he lives.

Gerald Killingworth

Lord of the Silver Hand

Matador
9 De Montfort Mews
Leicester LE1 7FW, UK
Tel: (+44) 116 255 9311 / 9312
Email: books@troubador.co.uk
Web: www.troubador.co.uk/matador

ISBN 10: 1 905886 01 2
ISBN 13: 9781905886012

Cover artwork: Laura Bradley

Typeset in 12pt Baskerville by Troubador Publishing Ltd, Leicester, UK
Printed in the UK by The Cromwell Press Ltd, Trowbridge, Wilts, UK

Matador is an imprint of Troubador Publishing Ltd

CHAPTER ONE

A Party

Caleb and Blossom knew they were safe.

A light had suddenly blazed on as their mother opened a door from the living part of the house where the party was taking place. She walked right underneath them. They were sitting on the first bend in the stairs near enough to have swung a foot and caught the top of her head or her ear, yet she had not noticed them.

With the door open, the noise of the party was much louder. Their parents' friends seemed to be laughing a lot and almost shouting. The children would have liked to creep up to the open door and peep in, but it would have been silly to risk being caught out of bed when they had something much more important to do.

They shrank down, putting their heads behind their knees as their mother walked slowly along the passage. She swung slightly from side to side in time to the jazz that could be heard from the dining room, and the long black lace sleeves of her dinner party dress swished floppily. Once they heard the crash of her blue Indian bangles as her arm hit the wall.

'I bet she's going to fetch that horrible big vase she bought yesterday. She's going to show it to Marion,' said Caleb when his mother had disappeared from sight.

They heard her rummaging in the junk room. There was a crash.

'There goes my bike,' said Caleb too loudly.

'Mum just said that swear word she shouted at you for saying.'

'I expect they're all sitting in there swearing,' said Caleb. 'I'm going to do it when I grow up. When mum's an old lady in a wheelchair, I shall visit her and swear all the time. *Eat your bloody tea, old lady* !'

'*I've got to bugger off now, granny,*' said Blossom copying him and then wishing she hadn't. What she had said made her want to laugh so much just when she couldn't make a loud noise. It was like swallowing an explosion or being at a party where you weren't expected to burp after drinking coca cola.

Mrs Belling-Peake came into view but without the vase. She had decided it was too awkward to carry. A long cobweb hung from the back of her piled-up hair like a ribbon.

'Sometimes I'm ashamed of her,' said Blossom.

They looked down on their mother's head again and wondered how anyone could not have guessed that they had an adventure planned for that night. They had been giving themselves away accidentally all day and she had not noticed a thing. The door of the dining room closed, muffling the noise of the party, and the children were left in the dark. They tiptoed quickly down the stairs and turned right along the passage where their mother had just been.

The ground floor of the house was divided into two parts. There was a big kitchen which opened onto the dining room which also had the settees and the television, and then, at the side of the house, were two other rooms where everyone kept junk they came across which they thought might come in useful one day or which was simply interesting.

Older junk tended to get buried under newer junk and it was exciting once in a while to excavate right through to the back and find the broken stirrup or the oil can with the instructions in Norwegian that you had completely forgotten about.

The junk side of the house had its own entrance, a side door with stiff hinges and a big stiff lock. Caleb had secretly been oiling these for the past week. This was a one-and-only chance expedition and they didn't want to be caught even before they left the house because their parents heard the lock or the hinges scream as they opened the door. They went out, locked the door behind them and pocketed the key.

The children were dressed only in their T shirts and shorts because it was extremely hot for a late October night. If they had put on anoraks, they would have suffocated. Everyone was talking about the weather. Whenever they eavesdropped on their mother on the telephone, she was always saying, 'I know, isn't it unbearable?' As if there could be anything wrong with weather that let you play outside whenever you wanted and in the pitch dark if you felt like it.

Now for the most risky part of the expedition, more risky even that walking on Hampstead Heath after ten o'clock at night. They had to go up the steps and across the path to the front gate. On account of the temperature out-of-doors, their parents' guests were likely to wander into the garden at some point. If any of them sat on the bench in front of the french windows, they were bound to see two absconding children with a duffle bag. Inside the bag were Caleb's binoculars, a star atlas, a torch, a camera with a flash, some bananas and a hammer for protection.

'We'll have to crawl under the laburnum,' said Caleb.

'I'm not crawling. You get slugs in the garden at night. Anyway, the path's always slimy. Mum will know we've been out because our clothes will be covered in marks.'

'Follow me,' said Caleb. 'On your belly till halfway and then sprint. I hope the last person left the gate open because I forgot to oil it.'

He was gone, leaving Blossom with the duffle bag. For a moment she thought of rushing back into the house, locking him out and eating all the bananas, but curiosity got the better of her. She did as her brother instructed.

In no time at all, it seemed, they were outside the front gate panting with relief and ready to carry out the exciting part of their plan.

CHAPTER TWO

A Meeting

Hampstead Heath was only minutes away. The whole family spent hours of the week there. Mrs Belling-Peake wandered up and down its hillocks and round its bushes, talking over to herself ideas for her children's books. She wrote under the name of Poppy Shandy, a name which Blossom and Caleb hated almost as much as their own names. Their mother believed in fairies and was often stared at as she wandered in a world of her own, tripping over roots and working out conversations and descriptions to put in her books. When she was dealing with a conversation, she did all the voices and gestures. The children always refused to accompany her, but sometimes secretly watched from a distance just to make sure that no-one from the local hospital took her away thinking she was mad. Their father they did not mind accompanying. He would shout, 'Time to walk the offspring!' as if they were puppies and they would scamper around him almost ready, you felt, to run after sticks or rubber balls. Their mother, sitting at the kitchen table surrounded by scraps of paper with notes on, her half-moon glasses at an angle, would look up sadly, recognising that she was not thought fit to join them.

So late at night it looked suspicious, two unaccompanied children headed into the blackness which lay on those wild square miles of countryside overlooking London. There were so many people about, Blossom and Caleb were terrified that a well-meaning neighbour would spot them and telephone their parents. The warm weather had drawn most of Hampstead into the streets and gardens; lights went on and off, cars drew up at the kerb. Caleb felt as if they were on a bombing raid and had to dodge searchlights. He took Blossom tightly by the hand and made her run a few steps and stop, pressed into a wall or hedge, and then run on again. Although she was silent she was enjoying it.

When they were actually on the Heath with darkness in front of them, no moon to speak of and invisible depressions in the ground ready to catch their feet, Blossom's courage faltered. She made a peculiar whimpering sound in her throat and said, 'We don't want to go too far, do we? What if we can't find our way back?'

Caleb had been expecting this and he had an answer ready.

'We have to go a bit farther to get away from the lights of the houses. We won't be able to see what's in the sky if we don't.'

'Switch on the torch,' suggested Blossom.

'It won't do much good.'

'Why not! You said you'd put some new batteries in it.'

'Yes I did, but I stuck crepe paper over the top.'

'Whatever for? You're supposed to make torches brighter not darker.'

'If we shine a bright torch on the star atlas and then look up into the sky, our eyes will be blinded. We won't be able to see a thing. It's a well-known fact.'

'It's a stupid fact,' said Blossom in her grumpiest voice. 'Can't we have the torch on anyway? And why didn't you bring another torch? You said you'd got it all planned out and you haven't.'

Caleb took the doctored torch out of the duffle bag and switched it on. The beam was no more than a suggestion of red, a faint blush on the grass, but Blossom was satisfied. They walked for about a dozen paces and then Blossom missed her footing, lurched, called out dramatically and stopped. She made the whimpering sound in her throat once more and Caleb began to feel annoyed. This might be the only chance he would have to see a comet for years and if his sister spoiled it all he had already prepared his revenge. He would tell their mother how Blossom and Pippa had drunk some whisky from the bottle in the dining room and how, when Mrs Belling-Peake had refused to buy her a new dress for a school party, Blossom had stolen a page of notes for her mother's story about the ladybird and put it on the fire.

'I'm not really frightened,' said Blossom unconvincingly, allowing herself to be led. 'I wanted to come ever so much.'

It was quite a long time before Caleb was satisfied that they had gone far enough. Their eyes had become used to the darkness which seemed less dense, although they could still not see where to put their feet. Behind them, the bedroom lights of Hampstead floated in the night. Directly ahead, where the Heath rolled and climbed towards Highgate, there was still a black wall, but the sky above was a dark grey. The butter colour of the street lamps, car head lamps, shop window lights, had seeped upwards making a haze in which disappointingly few stars were visible.

The comet was going to be very difficult to spot and Caleb expected that, if it proved impossible to locate, Blossom would need a lot of calming down. He would have to keep her busy, give her things to do.

'Let's sit down here,' he said.

'Shine the torch on the grass first,' said Blossom predictably. 'I don't want to sit in anything.'

'You don't get cows up here,' said Caleb wondering why people had to have sisters.

'No, but you get dogs and rubbish and the grass is all damp. Ugh.' She began to settle herself uneasily. 'It feels like a wet, hairy caterpillar rubbing against my legs.'

She leapt up again. She hated caterpillars.

'Stand up then, if you want,' said Caleb. 'I'm going to have a banana before I do anything else.'

Blossom loved bananas and was almost able to ignore the feel of the grass when Caleb gave her the biggest one to eat.

'Time please,' said Caleb who could have looked at his own watch but he wanted to stop his sister thinking about things like giant, wet caterpillars.

'Wait till I've finished,' said Blossom who was busy with the chunk of banana in her mouth. She flattened it with her tongue, bubbled spit over it and then piped it like toothpaste round all her teeth.

Caleb unpacked the duffle bag, realising that they should have brought something waterproof to lay the things out on. He was particularly concerned not to get his star atlas and the camera wet.

Patrick Moore had said that the comet would be best spotted some time after eleven and, if the sky were cloudless, might just be visible to the naked eye. Blossom, who was only interested in astronomy when it was spectacular, had been enticed along by the story that the comet would soar across the sky like a great firework. Caleb had not dared breathe the phrase, 'might just be visible to the naked eye,' to her and was wondering when she would ask, 'Where is it then?' and become difficult.

'Let's get our bearings first,' said Caleb turning to the appropriate page in his star atlas and moving it around so that the map of the sky matched the direction in which he was facing. His eyes moved upwards along the route of The Milky Way until they rested on the W-shaped constellation of Cassiopeia.

'This is going to be difficult,' he said. 'I'll have to lie on my back.'

'Why do we have to look at it now when we'll break our necks trying to see it?'

'It's so faint, you have to wait till it's as far as possible away from the lights of a built-up area.'

There, he had said the words 'so faint' and she had not jumped up and stamped around saying that he had brought her on a fool's errand. 'It should be somewhere between Cassiopeia and Andromeda,' he said.

'Why is it travelling between them?' asked Blossom. 'Why did it choose Andromeda where we can't see it?'

'It isn't and it didn't. The comet is inside the Solar System. The stars are outside it. They're the background. The comet only *appears* to be moving from Cassiopeia to Andromeda. It's actually moving from the fringes of the Solar system towards the sun and then it'll move out again and perhaps disappear forever. If you really want to know...'

'I don't,' interrupted Blossom quickly, but Caleb continued anyway.

'All the comets are part of a cloud of rocks and dust that surrounds the Solar System. Sometimes a passing star dislodges a bit and it falls towards the sun and becomes a comet.'

'You mean a star hits it, like kicking a football?'

'No. It's something to do with gravity.'

'You don't really understand all that,' said Blossom hitting the nail on the head.

'Yes I do!' retorted Caleb too violently to mean it.

'I'm so sorry, little comet, I seem to have kicked you out of your cloud. Silly old star that I am. There you go, whizzing towards the sun. Whee!' She unpeeled another banana.

Caleb swore.

'Oh can't you find it? It's on the bus to Cassiothingummy.'

'Those bananas will give you diarrhoea,' said Caleb.

'It's worth it. They're lovely,' said Blossom.

'Why don't the stars make sense? They're nothing like my atlas.'

'But it is good for ones so young to try and read the skies,' said a strange, deep voice and the top half of a man appeared out of the ground near them. The children felt a simultaneous cold wave shoot up their spines and make the muscles of their necks contract. Blossom's throat seemed to be flooded with banana and she thought she was going to choke or be sick. She couldn't move or speak or even breathe properly.

The Heath is crossed by a number of shallow ditches that are dry for much of the year. The tramp, which is what the children imagined the man to be, must have been lying next to them in a ditch they had not noticed, listening to their every word, biding his time to spring out. Caleb's fingers carefully reached towards the mouth of the duffle bag which contained the hammer.

'Do not be afraid, young ones,' said the stranger.

His voice made you want to listen to it and Blossom, whose mind was beginning to uncloud from its initial terror, wondered whether he was trying to hypnotise them. She couldn't stop herself wondering what it was like to be hypnotised and whether, if she were in a trance, she would believe she could fly and would even manage to do so like the stars floating through the Milky Way. Her mouth was creasing into a smile and she could not help it.

'You sit there frozen like rabbits before the fox, or grass dwellers before the snake,' said the stranger.

Then he laughed as he realised his comparisons might not be very reassuring.

'I am neither fox nor snake. Think of me more as the owl or squirrel.'

He laughed again and his laugh was both deep like a roll of distant thunder and breathy like a gust of wind through branches.

'I am Jack,' he said. 'You have seen my handiwork.'

He rose fully out of the ditch and sat very close to the children. His movement made Blossom sob and Caleb fell backwards and closed his eyes and prayed.

'Be not afraid,' said the stranger. 'I have come into your circle of light so that you shall not fear me.'

When the man had approached them, Caleb's hand involuntarily jerked away from the duffle bag. Now he moved it back and managed to slide two fingers into the mouth of the bag.

'So, you watch the skies. And what do you find there?'

'We were looking for a comet,' replied Caleb.

'Ah, yes. Those messengers and warners. It is fitting.'

His eyes glinted very brightly, unnaturally, and there seemed to be threads of silver in his hair although he wasn't an old man. He had on a very loose shirt that was probably green or light brown and his trousers were the sort you wore when you planned to do odd jobs. His sleeves were rolled-up and his long, thin fingers rested on his knees as he sat cross-legged. Caleb slid two more fingers inside the duffle bag. There was such a sharp glint from the man's eyes, such bright flashes as he blinked or changed the position of his head, that Caleb couldn't tell whether he was watching what he was doing.

'Have the last banana,' said Blossom after a brief silence in which the man looked first into her face and then into her brother's. At the moment their eyes met, both children felt that they were not looking at a solid face of flesh with lips, nose, hair, but beyond it through its diamond eyes to a confused landscape of leaves, mist and cold.

It was a chill picture but, strangely, not a frightening one. The moment of contact between his eyes and those of Caleb and Blossom was very brief, yet it seemed long enough to tell him, or possibly them, something important.

'No, I will not eat it,' said the stranger nodding at the banana in Blossom's hand. 'A strange fruit and not for me. I am made of sloes and dog-rosehips and blackberries.'

In other circumstances, the children might have howled with laughter at this eccentric remark, but at the moment it didn't seem in the least funny.

'I love blackberries,' said Blossom.

'Good,' said the man as if she had answered a question that had stumped the rest of the class, like knowing the name of the main river in Paraguay. 'I am Jack who can pinch all living things with my long fingers. But even Jack may seek help from children who look up into the skies and who like blackberries.' He sighed. 'Jack, Jack, where is your power now?'

Caleb had wormed his whole hand into the duffle bag. The mention of pinching with long fingers made it more urgent than ever for him to have the hammer.

'All is not well,' said the man. 'Beneath the earth all is not well. There is argument, rebellion, a disregard of duty. I have tried, yes I have tried, but it does not lie within my power. Perhaps you...'

Caleb slid the hammer down beside his leg where it could not be seen by Jack the lunatic, the escaped convict, whatever he was. As they had talked to the man, Caleb had relaxed and grown braver. His plan now was not simply to grab his sister and run off at the earliest opportunity. He intended to photograph the man if he could do it quickly enough and then to knock him out.

'If you were willing to come down there with me, what might we not see.'

'Down where?' asked Blossom who was beginning to feel comfortable and chatty.

The pained expression which had lingered around the man's mouth and eyes for a while disappeared as he threw back his head.

'Down where none of your kind has been for many a long year, young one,' he answered.

Caleb decided to act. Where did the man want to take them? Was it down into a cellar of peculiar people? It couldn't possibly be safe. He stood up, rather than jumped up, because kneeling in damp grass had taken away more strength from his legs than he expected. Shaking, he aimed the camera very inefficiently but at least he had the satisfaction of feeling the button go down and having to blink as the flash flared. Then, in a wild flurry of movement, he hauled Blossom to her feet and gathered their belongings. Even as he jerked this way and that, Caleb noticed very clearly that the man didn't move or make the slightest attempt to restrain them. He looked on like a spectator, the pained expression spreading back to every quarter of his face. When Caleb raised the hammer to bring it down on the man's head, the look in his intended victim's eyes took away his violence and his strength. How can you knock out someone whose eyes are saying, 'Why do you want to do this to me? I have not threatened or hurt you, have I?' When he let go of the hammer, it fell straight down and was absorbed by the grass in front of the stranger who remained seated.

'Come on!' said Caleb and the two children slithered and tripped their way to the lights at the edge of the Heath. They were not followed.

CHAPTER THREE

A Puzzle

They reached the car park at the edge of the Heath higher up than they had left it. Only the hammer and a banana had been left behind. Realising that *Jack* was not behind them and that, if they wanted to, they could scream and attract attention, they sat down on a verge to pull themselves together. Their hearts were pounding so much they could feel blood vessels throbbing near their eyes and in their arms. Their breathing was noisy and irregular. Caleb calmed himself down by re-packing the duffle bag carefully and pulling the string tight.

'Are you all right?' he asked.

Blossom had got up and swayed and sat down and fidgeted with her pony tail. Caleb was afraid she would faint.

'I don't think I'm going to be sick,' she said. 'I feel all tingly and there's something wrong with my legs. They won't walk properly.'

'Who was he?' asked Caleb.

'I don't know, but I wasn't really afraid. He didn't ask us for money or say anything rude, did he? I think he wanted us to go somewhere.'

'It didn't make sense,' said Caleb. 'Perhaps he was going to lock us in a cellar and then ask for ransom.'

'I don't want to think about it,' said Blossom. 'I thought he was rather nice. But they say the Devil can be very nice when he's trying to tempt you. If I told Miss Whiteside I'd met Satan on Hampstead Heath, she'd have me in detention for months. I don't want to know if he wanted to do something nasty to us. He made me think of things, sort of see things when he looked at me.'

'What things?' asked Caleb who thought he knew what she meant, but wanted to make sure.

'Oh, things. Good things. Sad things,' replied Blossom who couldn't find names for the brief pictures she had seen behind those sparkling eyes. They had been more like feelings than pictures. It was like trying to describe the smell or taste of bananas and she gave up.

'We can't tell mum and dad,' said Caleb. 'They'd go mad. They'd never let us out of the house on our own again.'

'It was our fault for going,' said Blossom. 'It wouldn't be fair to have mum go to pieces because we went out in the middle of the night. You remember what happened when you came off your bike and knocked yourself out. I've never heard anyone shriek like that before. She threw herself across you as if she was someone in a play. I wanted to hide.'

Suddenly she began to cry.

'Poor mum. What would she do if that man had kidnapped us?'

Caleb too felt a hot drop trickle down his cheek. He turned away.

'Well he didn't kidnap us and we'd better get back before we're missed.'

He walked off with a sniff, leaving his sister to follow.

It was round the hollyhocks and under the laburnum again and they were at the door of the junk side of the house. There was a moment's panic when Caleb thought he had lost the key which turned out to have hidden itself in a fold of his pocket. Once inside, safe and jubilant, they ran along the passage to the foot of the stairs, not caring about the noise they made nor whom they bumped into. They were inside the walls they knew so well and where they had parents to guard them and the only person who was likely to pop up unexpectedly was their mother's dippy friend Marion.

The next day was Saturday and the family was lethargic. Mrs Belling-Peake wandered about in her scarlet house-coat, her hair clumsily kept off her face by a scarf. She was trying to clear up the debris from the party, but, as she was not really awake, all she did was to move a wine bottle from the floor to the table or a plate from the table to a pile of several others on a chair. Then she sat down on one of the settees, closed her eyes and hoped someone would bring her a cup of coffee. The family were not very good at making her snacks and drinks and she expected she would have to stay there, fragile and with the beginnings of a headache, until she had the strength to put the kettle on herself. At the moment she didn't think she could face the squeak the tap made when you turned it on, the rattle in the pipe as the water came though and the tattoo it beat on the bottom of the kettle.

Mr Belling-Peake had received an early telephone call to do with his publishing work and was in his study where no-one was allowed to disturb him. Caleb and Blossom always assumed that 'Do not disturb' meant, 'I'm getting some private sleep,' which is what it would have meant for themselves.

The children came downstairs together, Caleb having knocked on his sister's door to see that she was all right. He was afraid the night's events might have left her peculiar, and she had had the same fears about him. When they saw their sleeping mother with her mouth sagging and one loose end of her scarf much longer than the other, they realised it didn't matter how many times they gave themselves away. Blossom was confirmed in her opinion that her mother needed a lot of looking after and she decided to make her some tea. When Mrs Belling-Peake was shaken awake, the first thing she saw was the cup of tea tremblingly offered by Blossom and the first thing she smelt was Caleb's disastrous experiments with the frying pan, eggs and lots of fat. Grey smoke drifted from the kitchen into the dining room.

'Oh no,' said Mrs Belling-Peake and closed her eyes again.

'I know you hate tea,' said Blossom, 'but I can't remember how to use the coffee filter. Would you like an aspirin?'

Nobody, not even Caleb himself, could have eaten the mess he had concocted in the frying pan. There was a huge amount of black and it was full of eggshell.

'Caleb darling, would you go and look for Marion. I'm not sure what happened to her last night. Someone might have taken her home. Or perhaps they didn't. Look in all the bedrooms, the cupboards and the outside loo. She does tend just to slump down in awkward places.'

Caleb left.

'No more, thank you. It was lovely,' said Mrs Belling-Peake giving Blossom her quarter-finished cup of tea. 'Are you sure you can manage?'

At all costs Blossom wanted to avoid thinking about what had happened the previous night. A good dose of housework would be just the thing. Feeling full of power, she took hold of her mother's slippered feet and lifted them so that Mrs Belling-Peake swivelled round into a lying position.

'Be a good girl and have a nice sleep,' said Blossom and went over to the sink to decide where to start work.

Caleb returned, having failed to find Marion.

'I don't want you here,' said Blossom.

She wanted to be alone, to lose herself in washing-up and tidying, jobs she normally avoided as much as Caleb did. Her brother was bound to want to discuss the strange man they had met and she didn't feel ready to do that yet.

'I was going to finish off the film in my camera, anyway,' said Caleb and went away.

After an hour, Mr Belling-Peake came in. He reminded Blossom how to work the coffee filter so she woke up her mother and gave her an orange biscuit and a mug of coffee. Mrs Belling-Peake was so pleased Blossom hadn't wrecked the kitchen, she said, 'After lunch I might show you the ideas I've had for the end of my new book.'

Blossom frowned. After all her hard work, she thought this was an insulting reward. If she met the ladybird who was the star of this newest Poppy Shandy book, she would drown it in her washing-up water.

'I may have to lie down after lunch,' she said imitating the invalid voice her mother had been using all morning.

'I thought,' said her father, 'that the whole family might prance around on the Heath this afternoon.'

Blossom frowned. Caleb was not there to support her.

'I had a very interesting phone call this morning from a chap who's got a splendid idea for a book about Ancient Britain,' said Mr Belling-Peake, not noticing that his only daughter was standing like a distressed waxwork, her coffee mug at an angle and the dark liquid slopping out. He ran his fingers through his grey-white hair and set tufts of it on edge all over his head like water spouts. His glasses bounced and moved down his nose. Although when he got excited, he looked as though he couldn't tell a cucumber from Christmas Day, he could still easily beat Caleb at tennis and golf even when he wasn't trying and Caleb was.

If they all went onto the Heath together, there would be safety in numbers, Blossom thought. Whoever heard of disreputable men kidnapping children when they were with their parents? She looked at her father's muscular legs, he often wore shorts around the house, and told herself that he could probably give the mysterious man a kung-fu kick if need be.

'Okay. We'll all go,' she said abruptly.

She took off her apron, threw it at a chair and missed.

'I'm going into the garden,' she said and went in search of Caleb.

At first her brother was nowhere to be found, so she sat on the bench in front of the french windows letting the hot sun play on her closed eyes. After about ten minutes, she felt something tickling the back of her hand. It would only be the tail of their cat Percy.

'I thought you didn't like spiders. There's a gigantic black one crawling up your arm,' remarked a voice.

Blossom shrieked, rose in the air and opened her eyes. The cat ran off and Caleb was standing in front of her laughing maliciously.

'You'll believe anything,' he said.

His sister bent down, picked up a handful of gravel and dirt and threw it into his hair. They were even.

'I've taken the film to the chemist's,' said Caleb.

He went over to the french windows and looked into the house.

'You mean *that* film?' asked Blossom when he rejoined her. 'When will you get it back?'

'On Monday. I told them I had to have the pictures for a very important school competition.'

'A picture of a man about to have his head bashed in with a hammer. Dad wants us all to go onto the Heath after lunch.'

'Mum too?' asked Caleb automatically.

'We've got to get used to going there again. We can't stay away from it for years and years until we're old.'

'Do you think *he*'ll be there?' asked Caleb. 'He's probably a weak old tramp and dad will beat him up if we tell him what he tried to do.'

'What did he try to do?'

'He said he had to take us down somewhere.'

'That's true. And he jumped out on us.'

'In the dark.'

'But he wasn't old and he didn't really seem like a tramp.'

        ~ ~

After lunch, Mrs Belling-Peake was amazed when both her children said, 'Go and put your walking shoes on, mum.'

'You and dad go,' she said. 'I'll stay at home and scribble a bit.'

They insisted she got ready.

They retraced their steps of the previous night and when they set foot on the first patch of grass the children felt their nervousness increase. Caleb led the family to what he thought was the spot where they had star-gazed but there was no tramp, no man with a sack hidden under his coat into which he popped unsuspecting children. Suddenly their mother, who had begun to talk to herself already, called, 'Look everyone!' A little way ahead of them, she was gazing at the shape of a star which was somehow marked in the grass. The blades inside the star shape were shorter and paler than those outside.

'How wonderful,' she said. 'It's going to give me hundreds of ideas for stories. I know it is.'

'A UFO landed,' said Caleb who knew at once that the star was a message.

'Vandalism. A practical joker who's been reading books about crop circles,' said Mr Belling-Peake.

'A comet crash-landed,' said Blossom and she and Caleb rolled on the ground laughing.

The star in the grass confirmed that the man they had met wasn't ordinary and that he hadn't meant them harm. Their Heath was returned to them and they could play on it as they wished with no fear of danger.

The family rambled on for a long time and Mrs Belling-Peake occasionally spun with pleasure that her children had made no attempt to abandon her.

CHAPTER FOUR

A Guest

On Saturday night, under the pretext of looking for some long-lost treasures, the children whispered together in the junk room until bed-time.

'The star's a sign from him. I know it is,' said Caleb.

'What does it mean then?'

'I haven't got that far yet.'

They went through the possibilities. The man was a refugee from a distant planet, he was a cannibal, an early April Fool joker sent by their friends - all these suggestions were equally likely.

On Sunday they both had homework to do and, when Monday arrived with its routine of getting up early and school, the excitement of Friday night already seemed an event in history.

Monday evening was black. Caleb tore to the chemist's for his photographs only to find a note stuck to the door saying, 'Sorry we had to close early.' There was further blackness when he arrived home. He and Blossom had hardly been at the kitchen table five minutes munching savoury spread on toast when Mrs Belling-Peake announced that there was to be a guest for supper.

'That means we won't be wanted again,' said Caleb.

'What a thing to say,' said his mother, shocked and worried in case he told all his friends and their parents that he was a rejected child.

'You remember how excited dad was about a possible new book on olden-days Britain? Well, today he saw the man who might be writing it and they got on so well dad's invited him to dinner. The man has a lot of translations of newly discovered Roman inscriptions, the thing dad's potty about. They plan to put together all the writings they can find about Britain in the days of the Romans as a sort of guide book. Isn't that a wonderful idea?'

'Is there any Marmite?' asked Caleb. Why did their mother always have to explain things as if she was talking to a five year old? She couldn't begin to know how much it annoyed him.

Mrs Belling-Peake persisted. 'The book will imagine that the reader is travelling all round the country by chariot or horseback or litter and will point out where to stay, with stars for the better hotels, amenities like baths and theatres and local customs worth seeing. But it will be set in 300 A.D.!'

'May I have a banana?' asked Blossom.

'Well *I* think it's a wonderful idea,' said their mother unsmilingly. 'And what's more, you're going to meet out guest.'

'Oh no!' said the children together.

'Oh yes. When dad told him he had two children, the man said he hoped we didn't mean to banish you from the dinner table. If he'd known what a charmless pair you are, he might not have been so anxious to meet you.'

'He doesn't *have* to meet us,' said Caleb. 'We can behave very badly when we want to.'

'You needn't try that. It won't be the first time you've been smacked in public,' said his mother.

'I've got too much homework,' I'm afraid,' said Blossom. 'I've got to write a nine million word essay about a ladybird.'

'Don't be sarcastic. You're only twelve and it isn't attractive,' said her mother whose temper was rising. 'Go and start your homework this minute and make sure you have thorough baths before dinner. We'll eat at eight o'clock and you needn't stay for the after dinner chat. It will all be about the book, I expect. Don't pull faces at me when you think I'm not looking, Blossom. And put that banana down. You've already had one.'

The children sulked off to make lots of mistakes in their French and History and Science as they always did when they were annoyed.

Shortly before eight o'clock, Mr Belling-Peake dragged his two reluctant children from their rooms. They knew better than to be obstinate and kick up a fuss because, when their father was angry, he was very angry indeed. They had bathed and dressed in their 'How nice to see you.' clothes and quietly, and absolutely coldly, they followed him into the dining room. Their mother was sitting on one of the settees talking to the guest and drinking whisky.

'Here they come,' she said in a high, unnatural voice.

'Don't be shy,' said their father who had to put his hands behind their backs and give them a hard push towards the guest who stood up to shake hands with them.

'Mr Frost, meet Caleb and Blossom,' said Mr Belling-Peake.

It was the man, their stranger from the Heath. Blossom knew that she had turned pale and her legs had sagged to one side.

There was no mistaking the man even though he was wearing a light grey lounge suit and was behaving exactly like someone who had an ordinary job and went to dinner with families he knew. Nothing, however, could dim the strange, shifting glitter in his eyes and hair, and those long, pointed fingers were different from any others in the world. Couldn't their parents see!

Blossom heard a whooshing in her ears and hoped she wasn't going to pass out.

How had he managed to be here in their own house, about to sit down to a meal with their parents and chat and smile with them? Caleb seriously thought of accusing the man of trying to kidnap them.

'They're charming but they seem a little over-awed,' said Mr Frost. He advanced towards the children who backed away and slightly irritated their father.

Then, with a darting glance, the man looked into their eyes and calmed them, let them know that they were to keep their secret. Once again, they saw, beyond his eyes, a distant country of mists and tumbling, curling leaves. The man stretched out his hand, first to Caleb and then to Blossom, and both children found that they were able to shake it without fear. Blossom, however, still kept a small suspicion that he was trying to hypnotise them and she made sure that she held his smooth, cool fingers for as short a time as possible.

'Sit with me and tell me all about yourselves,' said Mr Frost and ushered the children to the second settee, one on either side of him.

He began to ask them the kind of questions adults always ask children they are meeting for the first time - where do you go to school, do you have a favourite subject and so on. Then, when their mother went to have a last look at the meal and their father was checking the wine, their quest pressed a sharp fingernail into Caleb's left hand and Blossom's right and whispered, 'You have been chosen.' His finger nail left no scratch or dent in the skin, but they could feel the spot where it had touched them. It was as if they were sitting with an ice cube on the back of their hand.

Caleb wondered whether the man had deliberately given them a terrible disease by touching them and whether he ought to attack him. Blossom wanted to wash her hand and found that a tear had gathered in the corner of her eye. The man didn't try to help her understand what had happened and she began to hate him.

At the dinner table, the man soon said, 'Please don't call me Mr Frost. I'm James to my friends.'

'And you must call me Aldona,' said Mrs Belling-Peake.

The children groaned. It was always a bad sign when their mother asked to be called Aldona. She was bound to be silly. There was some talk of the book that Mr Frost and Mr Belling-Peake were considering and then the conversation turned to the unusually warm weather, as it did so frequently at that time.

'I have managed to find five soft, ripe apricots for our dessert on the tree in the garden,' said Mrs Belling-Peake. 'I never expected it would be hot enough to ripen the fruit, but it's as hot as August and all sorts of odd things are thriving in the garden when they ought to be dead. Doesn't that sound dreadful - telling living things they ought to be dead?'

'All creatures have their time for living and their time for going,' said the guest.

Caleb felt the ice cube spot on his hand tingle and he rubbed it. The man watched him.

'It's the end of the world, actually,' said Caleb by way of a diversion.

'Oh yes?' said his mother hoping her son was going to impress their guest with his imagination and not embarrass them all by talking nonsense.

'It's *The Greenhouse Effect*,' said Caleb and immediately lost his mother who had no idea what he was talking about.

Blossom yawned theatrically which made Caleb determined to blind them with science.

'There's too much carbon dioxide in the atmosphere. It comes from cars and factories. It forms a layer like the roof of a greenhouse and the world heats up. The polar ice caps will melt eventually and the world will flood.

'Rubbish,' said Blossom who hoped to live out her life without seeing the world drown.

'England will go under the sea,' continued Caleb. 'I want to stand on Hampstead Heath and watch the Post Office Tower submerge. Leviathan will swim up Haverstock Hill.'

'You don't know what Leviathan is,' said Blossom who had only recently come across the word herself.

'Yes I do!'

'Moderate your voice,' said Mr Belling-Peake.

'It's the greatest sea monster ever, with lots of heads and scales and fins and things and it's miles long. I want to see it swim by the house and look in Blossom's bedroom window. It'll recognise her as a close relation.'

'Caleb,' said his father warningly.

'Perhaps you *will* see it,' put in Mr Frost softly.

'Well, all I know,' said Mrs Belling-Peake is that it's very hot and five beautiful apricots have ripened. Their skins are as delicate as silk and I'm sure they'll be sweet and full of juice.'

She was not disappointed. The fruit was delicious.

'Lovely, but wrong,' Mr Frost said under his breath. Only Caleb seemed to have heard him.

After dinner, the children were sent to bed.

'I trust we shall meet again,' Mr Frost said to them when they wished him goodnight.

'I don't know,' said Caleb defiantly and shook the offered slim fingers very lightly.

The ice cube on the back of his own hand was suddenly more noticeable. An expression of anger, or pain possibly, wrinkled their guest's forehead.

The strange events of the evening were not over. The children couldn't immediately discuss their visitor because their father accompanied them upstairs to check that they brushed their teeth and got into bed. A suitable time after he had gone downstairs, Caleb crept into his sister's bedroom. She was tucking into a banana which she hid under her bedclothes until she saw who it was.

'I found this under my pillow,' said Caleb in a dry voice.

'The hammer you left on the Heath!' hissed Blossom. She stared at her half-eaten banana. 'I thought mum left this for me. *He* must have done. I've been poisoned!'

She threw the half banana into the furthest corner of the bedroom and covered her head with the pillows and a sheet.

'Go away, Caleb,' came a very muffled voice. 'I don't want to talk about him ever again. Go away!'

Caleb slunk back to his own room, turning over in his mind what Mr Frost had said to them.

It's all very flattering to be told, 'You have been chosen,' but, when you don't know what you have been chosen for and you have dark suspicions about the person who has done the choosing, it can make it a very worrying time.

CHAPTER FIVE

The Chosen

Next morning, when Caleb awoke, his left hand was resting against his face. He was aware of the cold spot next to his cheek and, although he went into the bathroom and held the back of his hand under the hot-water tap until it was no longer bearable, he couldn't warm that small patch of skin.

At breakfast, Blossom was at her most infuriating. When Caleb, pretending he wanted more Rice Crispies, leant towards her and whispered, 'Tonight,' she immediately put her fingers in her ears, closed her eyes tightly and shook her head.

'Caleb, not this early in the morning! Whatever are you saying to her?' asked Mrs Belling-Peake.

'A joke someone told me at school. She'd heard it before,' said Caleb full of panic.

He realised that Blossom was as safe as a tarantula or dynamite. She had to be treated with great care in case she blurted out their secret. All day at school he kept imagining the scene that might greet him when he returned home if Blossom failed to hold the secret in. But there was always the prospect of his photographs to bring him back to cheerfulness. After school he rushed to the chemist's where he had left the film. He flicked through the pictures of the house and of Percy the cat that he had taken on Saturday morning to use up the film. At first he thought that the picture of the man on the Heath had not come out. After a second desperate flick, he realised that it was the almost black picture with patches of grey that he had thought was a scrap of wasted film placed on top of the pile to protect the others. So that was that.

By the time he reached home he had decided that, if Blossom had been a traitress, he would lie and lie and then ransack her bedroom at a convenient moment. He was very disappointed about the photograph but not surprised. He took it from the wallet and tossed it towards the grille of the drain by the gate. At once he felt an odd sensation on the back of his hand and smacked it, thinking a fly or wasp had settled on him. The sunny days and the sticky, ripe fruit on bushes and trees everywhere had bred a large numbers of wasps. This was no wasp arranging itself to sting him, however. It was the cold spot where Mr Frost had touched him. He hadn't thought about it at school because the problem of what Blossom might say had taken all his attention. The tingling or stinging sensation came again. Caleb watched the photograph balancing on the bars of the drain. A puff of wind lifted it up and over the edge of the kerb to the side of his foot. Slowly, as if he were standing on an enemy, he put his foot on the photograph. The invisible wasp stung him again and he removed his foot from the photograph and stared down at it. Should he grind it with his foot or should he pick it up? He continued to stare, expecting his hand to be attacked by a swarm of unseen insects. Looked at from a distance, the photograph perhaps made more sense. Caleb bent down to retrieve it and pushed it deeply into his trouser pocket.

There was no earthquake when he walked into the kitchen, so he assumed that Blossom had kept silent. She had brought Pippa home for tea. Although Caleb couldn't stand Pippa, he was, in a way, glad, because having a visitor would take his sister's mind off Mr Frost and what he meant.

The girls were having a polite tea in the dining room and Caleb was told to stay in the kitchen. Mrs Belling-Peake had made them some thin sandwiches and allowed them to use her valuable teapot which held about a cup and a half. They were perched on the edge of the settee with napkins on their knees and taking flea-sized bites and sips.

Caleb went up to his room and leafed through the photographs again. He was proud of the ones of the cat; it seemed to be pulling faces at the camera, winking and putting its tongue out and in one there was a blur where it had turned round and wiggled its bottom. The Heath picture that looked like a disaster of the developer's art, he held at various distances from his eye and turned round and round because it was impossible to tell which edge was the top. The cold spot on the back of his hand was hardly noticeable now, thank goodness, and he was able to get on with his homework with the photographs spread out in a fan beneath the desk lamp.

At dinner, which was lasagne, Caleb didn't speak to Blossom. When she asked him to pass the the carton of grape juice, he shunted it across the table without looking at her at all.

'Did you have a good day at school?' asked his father.

'Not bad.'

'You may watch an hour's television if you like,' offered Mrs Belling-Peake.

' I've got things to do.'

'You said you'd finished your homework.'

'I have. This is something else. A personal project.'

After the meal, Caleb returned to his bedroom and waited. He packed the duffle bag with the hammer, his torch (without the red, masking crepe paper this time) some chewing gum and the apple and orange he had taken from the dinner table. He lay on his bed trying to concentrate on a *Superman* comic. From time to time, he picked up the photograph he had taken on the Heath and looked closely at it.

Perhaps he hadn't been sufficiently mysterious at dinner because it didn't seem that Blossom would come. He had counted on making her curious as he thought this was the only way he could give her the newest piece of information. If he had offered it to her outright, she might have gone into her fingers-in-the-ears-and-eyes-closed performance, or she might have let the secret out. Although he had more or less made up his mind what to do, he was a little frightened and wanted to ask her opinion.

At last she came.

'You were very rude pulling that face at Pippa,' she said not wanting to give away her curiosity.

Caleb didn't reply. He turned another page of his *Superman* comic and blew a bubble.

'Is that what you've been doing all night, reading your comic?' said Blossom suspecting she had been tricked.

'Three minutes before you came in I finished doing something very important.'

'What was that?' asked Blossom in a rush.

'You said you didn't want to talk about Mr Frost any more, so I'd better not tell you. That way you won't have anything to worry about.'

Blossom sat on his bed and swung her feet in irritation.

'We-ell,' said Caleb.

'Come on!'

'Look at this.'

He handed her the photograph he had taken on the Heath.

'This isn't anything,' said Blossom angrily. 'It's all black.'

'It's not all black,' said Caleb calmly and patiently. 'I've studied it for hours and I think it makes sense. What's that there?'

'A mark.'

'No. It's not a mark. What colour is it?'

'White. Grey. Cloudy.'

'That's right. And what's white, grey and cloudy and frightens people in churchyards?'

'Caleb, no!'

'No, I don't think he's a ghost. He's just come out on the photograph like a sort of ghost. The shape is the right height and those two marks might be his eyes or ears. Now look down here.'

He pointed to some pale, horizontal bars in the corner of the picture.

'They're wrinkles,' said Blossom firmly.

'I don't think they are. I thought they were wrinkles at first, but now I think they might be steps.'

'Steps! Gosh!'

Blossom held the photograph a couple of inches from her eyes and then at arm's length. She didn't want to believe that the lines were the edges of a flight of steps, but there was a clear possibility that they were.

'There aren't any steps there,' she said. 'It's only a ditch. We walked by it on Saturday afternoon.'

'There aren't always steps. But there must be steps sometimes, when Jack Frost needs them.'

'Jack Frost!'

'That's what he said his name was.'

'This sounds like something out of one of mum's stories,' said Blossom scornfully. 'It's as stupid as that ladybird. Ow, my hand!'

An invisible icicle had pricked the spot on her hand where Mr Frost's fingers had been.

'That happened to me too,' said Caleb. 'I threw the photograph down a drain and my hand kept hurting till I picked it up. When we're against him, he lets us know he doesn't like it.'

'I'm going to tell dad,' said Blossom who didn't feel safe. She got off the bed.

'Let's wait before we do that,' said Caleb. 'I think he only hurts us because he needs us so badly. It's only a pinprick. That's why I'm going back there. Tonight.'

Blossom sank to the floor and screwed up one of Caleb's comics as she thought what to do

'I can't go,' she said. 'I'd die.'

'Nobody's asking you to go,' said Caleb. 'When mum and dad have said goodnight, I'm going to slip out. If I'm not back in an hour, you're to tell dad.'

'You can't. You mustn't,' said Blossom looking up into his face and thinking she might never see him again.

'I'll be all right. Don't you dare tell them before I go.'

He knew what was going through her mind - if she ran to their father that very moment she could make sure he was locked in his bedroom every night. Blossom tapped on the floor with the rolled-up comic. The taps seemed to say, 'I shall tell. I shan't tell. I shall tell...'

'Only an hour, then. And you've got to let me know the exact moment you go and come back.'

'I'm taking the hammer. I can look after myself.'

'How did he get the hammer back in here last time?'

'I don't want to go into that. I'll get home in bags of time. You'll see.'

'I think I'm going to bed,' said Blossom and got up slowly.

Caleb stood in the doorway of his bedroom and watched her until she shut her door. If she tried to make a last minute dash downstairs to warn their parents, he imagined he would be fast enough to intercept her.

CHAPTER SIX

The Star

By nine-fifteen, Caleb was in bed and his parents had said goodnight. Neither said, 'Now what's this?' or, 'I don't mind what you've done as long as you tell me the truth,' which showed that Blossom had kept their secret.

At ten o'clock, his chosen time, Caleb retrieved the duffle bag from the wardrobe and searched amongst his discarded clothes for the T shirt and shorts he had worn on Friday night. He had got back safely when he last wore them and perhaps they would bring him luck a second time.

Blossom was asleep and had to be shaken awake. At first she wasn't aware it was her own brother with his face just above hers and his hand stopped her scream in the nick of time.

'I'm off now,' he said, disappointed that she wasn't dressed and waiting to go with him or at least offering encouragement. He was going to have to go onto the Heath alone with the distinct possibility that Blossom would fall asleep and not raise the alarm until morning if he didn't return.

'Don't you dare fall asleep,' he said.

Blossom was alarmed. She felt terribly tired and didn't think anything could keep her awake for another hour.

'Don't say that, Caleb,' she whispered. 'I don't think you should go.'

Caleb wondered how he could have imagined his sister dressed and eager, perhaps even shadow boxing to show how determined she was. He knew he had to leave quickly as she was on the point of breaking.

He had no difficulty in getting downstairs unobserved as his parents were engrossed in watching an interview with Marion on BBC2. They had the volume up very loud because they didn't want to miss it if she mentioned them or said something outrageous. He crept through the junk part of the house to the door with the well-oiled lock.

Once outside, Caleb paused and took a deep breath. How could Jack Frost know he was on his way, he asked himself. He hadn't thought about that before. He looked down at his left hand with the cold spot on it and said, 'I'm on my way, Jack Frost. Be there. Be there, please.'

A doubting voice in his head told him that people setting out on silly adventures looked even sillier when they tried to use the back of their hand as a telephone. The voice was silenced when the spot on his hand became colder and might even have glowed.

'Here we go then,' said Caleb and tiptoed to the garden gate.

He ran without taking any precautions to the edge of the Heath and paused there. With the torch in his left hand and the hammer in his right, and the duffle bag slung securely crossways over his back, he went to meet Jack Frost.

After some time, he thought he could see a brightness, a band of light, at the point towards which he was heading. The fact that this light was silvery green and not still, but had a kind of rippling or dancing quality, as if he was looking at the surface of a swimming pool on a bright day, made him uneasy. He couldn't bring himself to go nearer to the light and, instead, moved around it, approaching it from different angles like a sheepdog at work.

The doubting voice began in his head again. It said, 'Go home,' and, 'You shouldn't be here. It's dangerous.' The Caleb Belling-Peake voice, which argued against the doubts, said, 'Now you're here, why not go the whole way?' and, 'It's only a light.'

His own voice was just the stronger and he continued, although slowly.

The light was above the star in the grass which was sending up silvery-green phosphorescence in a spray about a foot high.

'Jack Frost?' said Caleb, his eyes darting all around him.

His words died away in the darkness and there was no reply. He waited and waited and the glowing star seemed to be fading.

'Jack Frost, I'm here!'

The glow had almost died and Caleb began to feel angry that, having come all that way, and having been so frightened, he was being turned away on the doorstep. Perhaps he ought to stand inside the star. He did this. At once the glow was rekindled and it began to rise. It rose, still in its star column, up to his knees and then up and up. He could have jumped out of the star, and a large part of him wanted to, but he had seen something which made him remain where he was. In fact, he had seen two objects, two feet, opposite him inside the star, and then calves and knees as the light danced higher. He couldn't run home and tell Blossom he had seen Jack Frost's knees; he had to see all of him. Hanging by the sides of the upper legs were the unmistakable long, thin fingers. Hands floating in space, hands that are probably not human and have no arms to anchor them, are not a reassuring sight. You half expect them to float away independently and to come at you from opposite sides like the hands of a puppet that can be made to come apart.

'Hurry up, Jack, this is frightening,' said Caleb. 'I don't like the dark.'

And Jack was there smiling.

'My young friend, it was a little test. Welcome. I shall not clasp your hand because mine is cold and there is a chill of fear upon you already. Be not afraid.'

'It *was* you in our home, wasn't it?'

The smile had already disappeared from Jack's lips and he had half turned out of the star. There in the ditch was the flight of steps Caleb was sure he had seen in the photograph.

'That's what you meant by *down there*.'

'Follow me, boy,' said Jack impatiently. He had a foot on the first step and expected Caleb to be close behind.

'I'm not going underground with you, just like that,' said Caleb firmly.

Jack Frost turned his head very heavily and then sank into a sitting position on the steps. He ran his long, shiny fingers through his hair which was so sparkling itself that you couldn't tell which was finger and which hair.

'I thought you had learnt to trust me boy. There is so little time and you have been chosen.'

'I do trust you - almost. But you do things so quickly. You don't give me time to get used to them.'

'Sit beside me, then, and question me as you will,' said Jack. 'When your heart is at rest, then you shall follow me underground.'

Still Caleb delayed. He didn't really think that sitting down by Jack Frost was like putting his head into a lion's mouth - and yet.

'Go home then, boy, if you cannot bring yourself to sit by me. Let the world flower and fruit until it sickens.'

It was a voice tired and angry at the same time. He spoke as if he were Noah looking out onto a world of water and saying, 'What could I do?'

'All right then,' said Caleb and sat down. 'First question. Who has chosen me?'

'You have been chosen. A youth and a maid. It is the way.'

'But who did the choosing?'

'It is the pattern of things. The stars *you* might say. That you had been chosen was clear. It shone from you.'

'You're speaking like someone from hundreds of years ago,' said Caleb who hadn't found the reply to his question at all clear. 'When you came to dinner you spoke properly. Why won't you speak like that now?'

'It was a masquerade then. I am myself now, or almost myself, and I must speak like myself. I am not human. You know that. Soon, with your help, and the maiden your sister's help, I shall look like myself.'

'With an icicle hanging from your nose,' said Caleb laughingly and immediately wished he hadn't spoken because two cold fingers pinched his arm hard.

'If you knew, if you knew, you would not jest,' said Jack.

'What seems to be the problem then?' asked Caleb, pretending that the pinch hadn't hurt him as much as it had.

'What can you tell me of the season?'

Caleb hated it when people answered questions with more questions.

'I don't understand you. Speak clearly,' he said anxiously. He wanted to help but it was no good Jack giving him instructions in riddles.

Jack sucked in his breath. He too was anxious and still half angry that he had to make use of a child who constantly asked for explanations.

'Which season of the year is it?'

'It's Autumn,' said Caleb, knowing he had the right answer.

'It is not.'

'It's October, though.'

'And Summer lingers. Do the leaves fall or do they not find new green? Are the days not hot and the nights also?'

'That's true,' said Caleb. 'But we're not complaining. We like it.'

'The year must go on, child. There cannot be Summer

38

forever. The earth must sleep. The swallows must fly. Sometimes we must extinguish the candle to save it.'

Caleb edged away along the step before he asked his next question.

'Aren't you doing your job then?' he said hesitantly.

'At last you see!' cried Jack clapping his hands together.

Caleb was confused. He thought he was being cheeky and yet it turned out that he had said exactly the right thing.

'I am not permitted to do my work,' said Jack, 'and so the year stays still. It rots in its fullness.'

'You want us to help you kill the Summer?'

Jack managed a thin, brief smile.

'Do not think of killing. Summer cannot die, but it must end for this year. Have I answered all you wish to ask? You do not know the danger I may encounter as we sit like infants playing on the steps of their home. Those below will know a door is open and bind me if they think I am working despite them.'

'Who are the people below?'

'Two great powers. Children merely, in many ways, and yet all-powerful. They wrangle and contend and so the Summer continues. They may have ears for my words even now and all may be lost. You little understand what may happen to your world above the ground if Summer goes on and on.'

'You weren't listening to me at dinner when I talked about *The Greenhouse Effect*,' said Caleb whose turn it now was to be sharp. 'The ice caps will melt and the sea level will rise and then where will we be? I know exactly what will happen.'

'I can tell you so much more in a secret chamber below,' said Jack. 'Come now. Danger lurks for us both here.'

'For us *both*?' demanded Caleb, suddenly very alert.

He had been won over to the idea of helping the strange man of silver, but he hadn't expected that there would be danger to himself.

'For you, very little danger,' said Jack in an offhand and unconvincing way.

'Do you promise I won't get hurt?' insisted Caleb. 'And Blossom too - if she comes.'

'I cannot make you that promise, little one. I say that if your courage is great you may well receive no harm. Who am I to promise that you will be brave? That is for you.'

'It's a deal then, I suppose.'

'I do not understand,' said Jack

'Good,' thought Caleb. 'I'm fed up with being the only one who doesn't understand.' Then he said, 'I will help you but I can't come down now because my sister Blossom is going to raise the alarm if I'm not back in an hour. Can't you come to our house again and talk to us then?'

'I think not. The gateways may be sealed against me. When I came to your house, I had no other choice. I was clinging to a sapling in a blizzard.'

'We talk about clutching at straws,' said Caleb who felt important and able to answer back.

Jack leant forward and stared from beneath wrinkled brows.

'This is no child's game, though I lean on the shoulder of a child.'

Caleb's spirit wilted.

'So you and your sister will return tomorrow?'

'We can't. Not in the middle of the week. What about Friday?'

'I do not always remember that your lives are not our lives. Be it Friday, then. And your sister shall come with you.'

'That may be a bit of a problem,' said Caleb. 'You frightened her and she's gone off the idea. Couldn't we come in the day-time? She wouldn't be frightened if it wasn't dark. We've both got half term all next week and we'll have masses of time.'

'Perhaps. Perhaps. The day-time is not good for me when I am powerless, for this is not my season. The apple still shines red and bright, as I mean to show you. Come both of you on Friday night and we shall plan together here.'

Jack pointed down the steps which dropped away for as far as Caleb could see.

'Is that a secret hiding place or an air-raid shelter?'

Jack chuckled. 'It is a palace, a kingdom. You shall see it in four days. Now our pact is made and, although I have little magic at this time, what I have shall be at your service. Take the weapon and the light and place them in your scrip.'

Caleb unhooked the duffle back and put the hammer and torch in it.

'Now stand in my star and close your eyes.'

As soon as Caleb closed his eyes, he lost his balance and pitched forward. When he put out his hand to steady himself, he scraped the ends of his fingers on a rough surface. It was the brickwork alongside the door of his home. He let himself in and crept to the foot of the stairs. His watch said a quarter to eleven and he could hear the sound of the television and the voices of his parents. Blossom was asleep which pleased him in one way, because he was too tired to give an account of what he had done, but, at the same time, he was annoyed. If his life had depended on her raising the alarm, then she had failed him.

He paid her back by leaving a note on her pillow. She would find it next morning and feel very guilty. It read, *I visited you at eleven o'clock last night but you were fast asleep. Signed, the ghost of your poor little brother. P.S. It was all right. Lots to tell you. Love Caleb.*

CHAPTER SEVEN

Underground

Caleb overslept and it took three calls from his mother before he had the strength to open his eyes completely and tumble out of bed. He had his underpants half on when Blossom burst into his bedroom to tell him that his breakfast was stone cold and that he was bound to be late for school.

'Get out and stop peeping!'

Blossom tried ineffectually to whisper through the hinges of the door as he finished dressing and took his time brushing his hair. When he came out of the bedroom he walked straight past her without saying a word. She followed him down the stairs wanting to shake him.

'What happened?' she asked several times.

'All will be made clear this evening, my dear,' he said.

He was going to make her stew all day. That would be her punishment for falling asleep when he might have been in mortal danger.

That tea-time, as Blossom sat at the kitchen table munching toast and honey, she couldn't take her eyes off Caleb. She was eating blind and once she pushed a particularly gooey square of toast into her hair as she concentrated on Caleb rather than on what was going into her mouth.

Unusually, their father was having a cup of tea with them.

'Dad,' said Caleb, 'what's the opposite of *human*?'

'Why?'

'We were talking about it in English.'

'You could have *super-human*. Someone who has extraordinary powers is superhuman.'

'Like superman?'

'I suppose so. Then there's *sub-human* which means less than human. A monster or an ape-man perhaps. *Inhuman* means more cruel and ruthless than a human being ought to be. And there's *non-human* which simply means that a creature is not human, but could be anything else besides. You could astound your English teacher by offering him *pseudo-human* - pretending to be human - or *infra-human* or *crypto-human*.'

'I think I like *non-human* best,' said Caleb.

He had found what he wanted - a word to describe Jack Frost. Jack had spoken of himself as not human and Caleb was afraid to think of him as a sub-human monster or a super-human power pack. *Non-human* was the most manageable word. It simply meant that he was not like other people and it didn't make you too uneasy. He was someone else – that was all. *Non-human*. Still, it was an exciting thought. Did it mean that he would live forever and never grow old?

'I'm going to look at my bike,' said Caleb casually.

Blossom took a mouthful of air instead of orange juice. She knew that Caleb wanted to talk to her in the junk room.

'Don't slurp, darling,' said her mother. 'Remember how nicely you ate your tea with Pippa yesterday. Caleb, change out of your uniform before you go near that bicycle.'

In less than five minutes, brother and sister were in the furthest corner of the junk room with the door closed behind them.

Caleb gave an account of what had happened to him the previous night, although neither he nor Blossom could honestly believe that he had been spirited home by magic.

'Those steps really went down into the ground and he said there was a palace and a kingdom under the Heath,' repeated Blossom for the third time, overcome with excitement.

'I've told you,' said Caleb. 'We've got to help him, both of us.'

'I might be busy.'

'Don't be daft. Still, I don't see why I can't do it on my own. I'm much more reliable. At least I wouldn't fall asleep if I was left on guard.'

'That was only once,' declared Blossom. 'I had a bad headache. I had to take an aspirin.'

'I bet. On Friday night he's going to tell us the plan and then we have half-term next week to carry it out. I'm always going to take the hammer with me in case we have to break out.'

Caleb saw himself smashing down doors with one mighty blow.

'We'll have to find you a weapon too,' he said.

Blossom's picture was of herself at the head of an army, her long golden hair swirling in the breeze and a silver spear in her hand. She would be worshipped by everyone. They would lay down their lives for her.

'I think we'll need to get into training,' said Caleb. 'What do the London Marathon runners eat for their special diet?'

'What do weight lifters eat, more like,' said Blossom seriously.

'Yes, we might need to fight. Our training starts this very minute. No late nights and no television because it'll make our eyes go fuzzy.'

'Do you think we ought to go for runs?' asked Blossom.

'No. We can eat sweet things like toffee and barley sugar because sugar gives you energy.'

Blossom took her training very seriously. At school, she rested as much as she could and refused to play catch with Pippa and Rosemary and the gang at lunch times because it would tire her unnecessarily. She tried unsuccessfully to climb a rope in gym in case they fell down a well and someone

44

lowered a rope to them, and she ate plenty of Mars bars and packets of M&M's to keep up her blood sugar level.

At last Friday night came. After dinner, they told their parents they were going to bed early as they wanted to play on the Heath all day Saturday.

'Stocking up on your sleep for half-term, eh?' said their father. 'Does that mean mum and I can watch what *we* want on the television for once?'

The children let this unfair remark pass.

Ten o'clock, as usual, was the time chosen for breaking out. The duffle bag once more contained the torch, the hammer and fruit and a ball of string. Caleb had lain in bed conserving his strength for later, dozing and, in between dozes, trying to think what he ought to take for a visit to an underground country where he might encounter magic. He was hoping that he would automatically assume magical powers as soon as he was inside that other world. He wondered whether it had a name.

They had no difficulty getting out of the house and were soon on the edge of the Heath. Blossom had by then recovered from the rude remarks Caleb made when he saw how she had dressed for their visit to Jack Frost's palace. She had thought her long blue skirt and her white blouse with all the frills and granny's silver brooch would be exactly right for a royal visit. She had turned against the idea of herself as a warrior and preferred to be thought of as *The Princess Blossom, lovely as the morning* and whose beauty passed into legend. They were bound to give her a crown to wear down there, she felt. Nobody she had ever seen had hair as naturally golden as hers. She tried not to be big-headed about it. Caleb had all but ripped the clothes off her.

'There might be a war going on down there,' he told her. 'There probably is from what Jack said, but he speaks in riddles. Go and put some proper adventure clothes on or stay at home.'

Blossom put on her T shirt and shorts and prayed that the people they met underground would recognise that she was a princess and not a prince with a pony tail.

The star in the grass was glowing silver-green as before and Caleb told Blossom to stand in it next to him.

'Watch this,' he said and almost at once the dancing lights lapped around them and Jack's feet appeared.

'She came,' said Caleb full of himself, but, as soon as the light had reached the topmost point of Jack's hair, Jack turned without a word, without a *Welcome,* a *Glad you could make it,* or even a *Follow me.*

The children went after him obediently, although they thought he was being very ungrateful.

The steps, which were plain and dusty, and not what you would have expected to find in a palace, descended for a long time, turning on a gradual spiral as they did so. The walls were of a smooth, natural earth with irregular streaks of sand and gravel in the darker background of ordinary soil. It was cool and there was no damp, earthy, ditch-like smell. The light was gentle and variable. It was provided by coloured crystals set in the walls at different heights so that, sometimes, the children could see the earth curving above their heads and, at other times, only the surface of the steps was lit.

As he descended, Jack made no allowance for legs that were shorter and younger than his. He never broke into a run, but, occasionally, he would take two steps in a single pace. Caleb and Blossom were in unfamiliar territory and didn't have the courage to call for him to slacken his speed.

They were hot and breathless and a great way from the surface of Hampstead Heath when the staircase came to an end.

'Keep close to me,' said Jack harshly as if they were soldiers.

They hadn't seen his face for many turns of the stair and they would have been happy to cling to the back of his shirt because a large number of very small passages led off from the bottom of the staircase like the complicated insides of someone's lung. When Jack moved suddenly sideways, it was not even into one of these passages that he led them. What appeared to be a dark zig-zag in the earth wall turned out to be a slim fissure into which Jack slid.

'Here!' he said, as if they had changed from soldiers into slaves.

He moved so quickly that the end of the word was spoken with his body already in the fissure and there was an echo.

'Come!' said the echoing voice again, like a voice in a dream.

The children followed and found themselves in another passage. Their journey was now along passages that twisted and turned and they realised they were completely in Jack Frost's power. Without him, they had no chance of returning to the surface. It was a thought that occurred to both of them, but it was too frightening to be put into words.

The end of their journey was unexpected.

'We are here,' said Jack at a random point in the wall. There was no doorway and the children couldn't understand why he had stopped.

'Don't leave us!' said Blossom who was overwhelmed by the possibility of being trapped there for ever with thousands of tons of earth between them and home. Jack had passed into the wall and was gone. The children stared at the spot where he had disappeared, hoping that hinges and door panels would miraculously appear. The wall remained earth.

'Think! Think!' said Caleb to himself. 'He wouldn't just leave us. We're too important. I know he wouldn't.'

As he tried to work out what to do, he knocked his head with his clenched fist. Then he looked closely at his fist and suddenly lashed out with it at the wall. It went through and came out on the other side, or, at least, into an open space.

'Pull your arm out, Caleb. It's eating you. The wall's alive,' shouted Blossom wildly.

'I can't,' said Caleb who could feel long, cold fingers clasping his hand tightly.

'He's got me. He's pulling.'

And Caleb disappeared too, with the speed of a bubble bursting. Blossom managed to stay sufficiently clear-headed to tell herself that no-one ever escaped from a tunnel by weeping and wailing. She would have to follow Caleb. There was no going back and there was no staying where she was. She thought of huge earthworms or leather jackets squirming through the tunnels and opening their ugly jaws and chomping her up, or simply not noticing her and squashing her. Experimentally, she tapped the wall with her sandal and half an inch of the toe disappeared. She instantly pulled it back. There was no way of telling how thick the wall was and she dreaded walking into it and ending up with one arm and a leg on one side, the second arm and leg on the other side, and her head, nose, mouth in the thickness of the wall where she would suffocate. Caleb wouldn't allow this to happen to her. Why hadn't he returned to give her support? He was being held prisoner! No sooner had this thought come to her than she struck the wall harder than her brother had done. There was the same feeling of space around her hand, the grasping by the cold fingers, the pull and there she was beside Caleb.

'He wouldn't let me help you,' said Caleb with an unfriendly emphasis on the word *he*.

'I am Jack, not *he*, and her resolve had to be tested. She has courage, I can see. I hope not to test her again. Sit.'

They were in an oblong room with its low ceiling, its walls and its floor all of smooth earth. Set into the walls were the glowing stones the children had grown used to as the source of light. Now that they were sitting still on a pile of fleeces, they had more time to take notice of these stones. Some were as clear as glass and green; others were whorled or murky like treacle and gave off a warm brown glow for a few inches. Some were no bigger than sequins.

'This is my thinking room,' said Jack who squatted at the end of the pile of fleeces. 'As you were expected, I prepared it to receive you. We are almost safe here. It is my magic that enables us to pass through the walls. If others try, the walls will cast them back.'

'Some room. Some preparation for guests,' thought Blossom who had hoped for gold and silver everywhere.

It was no more than a block cut straight out of the earth. You could make just this sort of *room* with about three cuts of your spade in the wet sand at the seaside. And the fleeces had been thrown into a corner any old how, although she admitted they were comfortable and had a sleepy smell.

The only other furniture was a rough wooden table supporting a flagon and three beautiful goblets.

'You're not friendly any more, Jack,' said Caleb. 'We're not very old.'

'I know that, boy.'

He ruffled Caleb's hair and made him shiver.

'I am your friend. Be not mistaken. I am the friend of all your kind. That is why I do not trouble to bow and smile at you. Please understand how little time there is. I cannot yet see how you will be of use, but you have been chosen and a way must be found. I shall tell you all. But first, a drink.'

He got up and went over to the table where he poured a clear, yellowish liquid from the flagon into the goblets. He handed a goblet to each of the children and kept one for himself.

'It is from apples,' he said.

'Cider,' said Caleb. 'I like cider.'

'You will find it better than cider.'

Blossom was captivated by the goblets. They had a short stem and a wide, shallow dish and were made of bronze. The pattern on them was of intertwining stems and leaves made of gold wire and, at intervals, there were flowers of red enamelwork.

Caleb was sitting between Jack and his sister and, when he raised the goblet to his lips, Blossom was in a position to see Jack's eyes above the rim of the bronze vessel. They were wide open and unblinking as if he were waiting for something very important to happen.

'Don't drink, Caleb!' shouted Blossom and knocked the goblet from his hand. The juice went everywhere.

'What did you do that for? I like cider.'

'I bet it wasn't cider,' she said, putting her own goblet down carefully. 'Was it Jack?' She turned to Caleb. 'You remember the story of Persephone? She ate some pomegranate seeds when she was in the Underworld with Pluto and she had to stay there for ages.'

Caleb gulped and Jack gave part of a smile .

'If we had drunk that, we'd have had to stay here, wouldn't we?' continued Blossom. 'You know that's true and you can't deny it. You're not fair. I don't think I'm ever going to like you.'

Jack didn't look at all ashamed of what he had tried to do, which Blossom thought was shocking.

'You have been tested numerous times and not been found wanting,' said Jack. 'It is right that you were chosen. You have courage and you have your wits. Your liking me does not matter.'

'That wasn't a test,' said Blossom. 'You were trying to play a nasty trick on us. You wouldn't have let us go.'

'In time I would. When the task was done.'

Blossom was silenced by this confession. She had already said enough to impress her brother.

'Can we have the story, please?' asked Caleb. 'We didn't drink that apple stuff, so I want to go home and have a bath. I'm all sticky with juice.'

Jack began.

'Perhaps you wonder where we are,' he said. 'This is a forgotten corner of the realm of Lud and Brigantia.'

Blossom opened her mouth.

'They are the king and queen here, child. There will be no need for questions. I shall make all clear. These rooms are never needed or visited and I am safe here to make my plans. Later, you will go into the palace. It is rich and beautiful. At the centre of our kingdom is a grove with a single apple tree on which grows a single apple. As the time comes for Summer to draw towards its end, Brigantia, the queen, she who tends the grove, picks the apple. With my icy fingers I pinch its skin and so the Autumn begins. My magic grows apace then. Mine is the power. I roam the countryside bringing sleep beneath my frosts and chills.

'Lud, the king, and Brigantia, his consort, have quarrelled. Even they cannot name the cause. All Spring they glared and were silent and then, in the height of Summer, the words sprang forth from their mouths. Such unforgivable words. King Lud stole the apple and hid it where not a soul but he can tell where. And the Queen Brigantia stole his silver hand as he slept.'

'His sil...,' began Caleb.

'Yes, his silver hand. Many centuries ago, before your own ancestors had come to this island, he began another quarrel with his brother Belenos whose flame is your sun. Their strife was long and bitter and, as they struck savage blows at each other, Lud's hand was lost. The sword of Belenos, coming from below, severed it and sent it high into the air where the flames of the sun burnt it to ash. When they were reconciled, had kissed and promised never more to fight, Belenos asked Goibniu, the smith of the gods, to fashion his brother a new hand of silver. It is with this hand that he summons the rainstorms of Autumn and so is called *The Cloudmaker*. Brigantia, in revenge for the theft of her apple, or perhaps the hiding of the apple was revenge for the theft of the hand, has hidden the hand I know not where. There is no apple and there can be no clouds. The Summer lingers. While their quarrel lasts, the seasons never alter and if, by Samhain, we have not found what is lost, my power will be gone for ever and Autumn and Winter will come to you never again. Lud is my master, but, when I have pinched the apple, I am lord of the land. They must not know of my work now or imprisonment may be my lot and all will come to naught. Imagine Jack, the silver strider over hedgerow and down, the hanger of jewels of frost, the nipper of noses, confined in an earthy bed with not a single breath of winter storm upon him.'

'What's Samhain?' asked Blossom.

'The turning of the year. The proper end of all warm days. If Summer lasts beyond Samhain, then the sequence is broken for ever. Comets will abound and Belenos will blaze in the sky till the end of all things. Samhain is the feast you call *All Hallows*.'

'Hallowe'en! That's the end of next week,' said Caleb. 'Crumbs. Can't you tell them they're being silly and thoughtless and they ought to behave themselves?'

'Soon you will cast your eyes on King Lud and Queen Brigantia and you will understand why I keep my peace until I come into my strength. My magic at this time is more slender than the waned moon and I am their plaything. I am Jack the servant, not Jack the master.'

'Why do *we* have to search for the apple and the silver hand?' asked Caleb. 'I'm sure you've got a much better idea of where to look.'

'It is in the nature of things. You have been chosen. I would not have chosen children from the upper world, you know that, but it is clear that to your eyes alone will what is lost be revealed.'

'Where do we begin our search?' asked Blossom.

'That is yours to discover. The apple and the hand could lie in your world or ours. Never rest from the search. When you have listened to the king and queen, you will know more.'

'Listened to them!'

'I cannot come near them when they rage. They call down curses on each other and their attendants shrink in fear. It is my notion that you join their trains and listen, listen. But have a care, There are those who will be against you, who revel in this dissension and bask in the sun. They will be glad to see Winter banished and Jack Frost with it. They would play in the sunshine for ever, fools that they are. You must entrust your thoughts to no-one. When you come again, I shall have apparel for you.'

'Costumes!' said the children together.

'You must look like children of the palace, not of the upper world. Your speech, your manners, all proclaim what you are. You must speak little for I have no time to train you.'

'We're going to be spies,' said Caleb. 'Whoopee.'

'In fairy stories, children have a magic charm to protect them,' suggested Blossom who was hoping that Jack would take from his pocket the most beautiful gold bracelet or ring she had ever seen.

'This is no tale,' said Jack dismissively. 'I despair. They will see that you are my creatures instantly.'

'No. No,' insisted Caleb. 'We'll be perfect. We'll try ever so hard. When do we start?'

'You will come tomorrow in the daylight for time is short. There is danger if the gates are opened with the eyes of Belenos over us, but who are we to choose?'

'We'll be at the star at ten o'clock sharp,' said Caleb. 'Now I think you'd better let us go.'

'All those steps,' sighed Blossom who was extremely comfortable on the pile of fleeces.

'I have saved some of my power for this,' said Jack. 'Take my hands, cold though you find them.'

When the children were clasped on either side of him, he lifted them off their feet and threw them forwards. Far too fast for it to be clear what was happening, they spun and tumbled through walls and along passages and finally shot up the flight of steps to arrive dizzy and befuddled in the ditch by the star. Caleb said he felt as if he had escaped from a submarine and Blossom insisted she would always have sympathy for the clothes in a washing machine from now on. When their heads cleared, they dragged their tired bodies home.

CHAPTER EIGHT

A Last Week

Mrs Belling-Peake had the unusual experience for a Saturday morning of hearing her children storming up and down the stairs at 8-30 calling, 'Come on, mum, we want our breakfast so we can play on the Heath all day.'

She had spent the night being Poppy Shandy and trying to think of amusing incidents for the next chapter of her ladybird story. This left her tired and vague. She wasn't sure whether she was still in her dreams as Caleb and Blossom shouted all over the kitchen, 'I said *not* milky tea,' 'This egg's cold,' and so on.

'We've got to have some sandwiches,' said Caleb, 'because we won't be back for lunch.'

'You're big enough to make your own sandwiches and there's plenty of fruit.

Blossom got the sliced bread and began to spread it.

'Whatever are you mixing with that Marmite?' asked her mother a little later. 'No, don't tell me.'

'Hurry up or we'll be late,' said Caleb.

They threw the food into the duffle bag and left the house.

If Mrs Belling-Peake had been able to think more clearly, she would have asked, 'Late for what?' and tried to prevent their going out of the house in such grubby clothes. They had on their lucky shorts and T shirts again.

'I don't expect for one second you noticed me take this,' said Caleb as they walked through the garden. He drew the bread saw half out of the duffle bag.

'What do you want that for?'

'It's a weapon. It's in case. I took it from right under mum's nose.'

'It's got those silly teeth. How can you hurt anybody with that?'

'I could saw their hands off. I won't ask you to show me your weapon because you forgot all about needing one.'

'No I didn't!' shouted Blossom angrily. She was lying. 'You kept hogging the duffle bag so I had to leave my weapon in my bedroom. Give me that!'

She snatched the duffle bag and rushed back into the house. When she reappeared, she said, 'My weapon's a secret. It's in here and you're not to look at it till we need it. That'll serve you right for thinking you're so clever.

It was 9-30 and they had plenty of time to keep their appointment with Jack Frost, but they walked along the road far more slowly than people who don't have to hurry. It was an attack of nerves, really. In the kitchen, they had rushed around and demanded, but now they were on the verge of a visit to the palace under the Heath, they had time to think of all the dangers it might involve. Blossom remembered how she had felt in the underground passage such a short time before.

'Caleb, I don't know about this,' she said. 'We're going to meet *them*. Do you think they could turn us into something terrible?'

'Of course not. Jack would stop them. He'd freeze them to death.'

'His magic's not very strong yet.'

After this not very encouraging conversation, they quickened their pace but, once on the edge of the Heath, they became slow and reluctant again. The duffle bag slipped from Caleb's shoulder and he allowed it to drag along the ground behind him. They found it impossible to direct their steps towards the star in the grass and, despite the fact that ten o'clock came and went, they continued to roam in great circles, afraid to begin their adventure.

Summer was still everywhere. It was only as they rambled in no particular direction that they truly noticed it for the first time. Swallows dived and played in a sky that glowed and had no feel of Autumn. When the sun dips towards Winter, you can tell because the rays strike the earth at a different angle. Your eyes register the change at once: a sharpness and a thinness of the light. Blossom looked around her. It was definitely still Summer light.

'You *can* tell,' she said. 'There *is* something wrong.'

'It's all so green,' said Caleb. 'You feel as if you ought to be going to the sea.'

'Or Wimbledon. I didn't pay any attention when mum kept going on about the swallows not bothering to leave us this year. She said somebody ought to tell them before it was too late and the cold trapped them.'

'They knew the cold wasn't going to come. Look at those leaves. They're only just unfolding.' He struggled to break off a switch. 'These twigs are sappy and bendy. They usually snap more easily about this time.'

'And bees and wasps,' said Blossom. The Heath was so comfortable and lovely she wanted to lie in the thickest grass she could find and look up at pure white clouds or just doze and try to work out what the noises were she could hear. Anything was better than creeping along tunnels with mud walls and ending up turned to stone by a king and queen who should have known better.

The spot where the star in the grass lay was out of sight as they had, without thinking, kept one of the gentle rises of the Heath between them and it. Every once in a while, either of them would look up to the horizon and think, 'It's there. Just over the brow. When dare I go?'

'Jack will wonder where we've got to. I'm surprised our hands haven't started tingling,' said Caleb swinging the duffle bag at the edge of some bushes that formed a skirt around a couple of trees.

'Jack has been waiting these many minutes,' said a voice from behind the bushes and a head appeared.

It was a relief that Jack had suddenly arrived because now they would have to go with him. He had made their decision for them.

'Sorry,' said Caleb. 'It was hard coming.'

'I must not be seen by the bright eye of Belenos. Come over to me,' said Jack. 'Jump here.'

He pointed to a dark patch of shade between the bushes and the children jumped towards it. Only it wasn't a patch of shade; it was a hole, a sort of tunnel and slide combined.

CHAPTER NINE

The Palace

Blossom was surprised and relieved that their downward whizz didn't end with them tangled up in each other and their arms and legs broken into pieces an inch long. She seemed to be upside down or spread in a star like a parachutist every other minute as they made their unusual way into Jack's secret chamber.

So there they were, sitting comfortably on the floor with their legs stretched out in front of them and not a trace of that *My stomach is floating yards above me* feeling you generally get when a fast lift stops.

The room was much the same as before: the earthen walls with the crystals which produced light, the rough table, the pile of fleeces and, in a corner, some bits and pieces which probably meant that Jack was spending more time there.

'I enjoyed that really,' said Caleb.

'Wait for me,' said Jack. He didn't get up and leave the room which is what you expect people to do when they tell you to wait. Instead, he dragged himself with difficulty over to the fleeces and sat down, his head hanging. His arms rested stiffly on his lap and his eyes were closed.

The children watched in bewilderment.

'Don't die!' shouted Blossom as Jack showed no sign of reviving.

'I hear you child,' he said after a while and raised an arm to rest it on the table.

'Are you ill?' asked Caleb who shared his sister's fear that, on a bright, warm Saturday, they had stepped into a grave.

'You are not easy children to manage. You tire me. It took much of my power to move the gate of Lud's kingdom from the star to where you found me. Why are the children of Men so headstrong?'

Blossom looked across at Caleb as if to say, ' There's not much he can do to us at the moment.'

Jack followed her eyes. 'You register my weakness, I see,' he said.

'What do you want us to do, Jack?' asked Caleb.

'I have to transform you.'

Blossom's vision of herself as a princess danced before her eyes again.

'On the floor, there. Bring me the garments.'

The children rushed to gather up the two piles of clothes which they had not paid any attention to. What delighted them most was the jewellery: brooches, rings and bracelets on top of the woollen dress for Blossom, and the tunic and trousers for Caleb. They looked enviously at the coloured enamels on each other's ornaments and then carried them to the table next to which Jack had slumped down again. He carelessly brushed Blossom's gold ornaments onto the table top as if they were rubbish.

'This is the long garment worn by womenfolk,' he said roughly unfolding a dress of pale blue wool.

Blossom almost stamped with impatience. Of course it was a dress, anyone could see that. Why didn't he get to the thin circlet of gold with the red stone at the front that had been folded into the dress? She was dying to put it on.

'Pin the cloak at this shoulder. This is for the arm and this for your finger.'

Jack left out the beautiful circlet which Blossom picked up in any case. He placed his fingers around it as if he were going to take it away from her, but Blossom's fingers tightened obstinately.

'Wearing this, you will not easily hide yourself,' said Jack.

'I don't care.'

'So be it.'

'Where can I change?' she asked.

Jack flicked his hand. Blossom at first thought this was a gesture of impatience until she realised that he was pointing towards the far wall. Naturally, there was no door there, but, rather than ask a a silly question and get a rude answer, she purposefully walked up to the wall and then passed through it. When she re-emerged, heavy with gold and already beginning to itch because of the wool next to her skin, she found Caleb kneeling on the floor with his head in a large bronze cauldron and Jack hunched over him, his hand on Caleb's neck.

'Stop that!' shrieked Blossom and she flew at Jack who appeared to be drowning her brother.

'Away!' said Jack. 'Or I shall blind him.'

Blossom raised her arms high and wished her fingernails were longer. When she threw herself at Jack, he swung her up on his arm while still managing to keep Caleb's head in the cauldron. Blossom, numbed by the coldness of Jack's body, was slowly lowered to the floor as Caleb's head, like the other end of a see-saw, emerged from the milky water of the cauldron.

'Caleb!'

'He's only doing my hair. Shut up!' her brother shouted back.

Blossom backed away to take in some deep breaths and to allow herself to calm down. She could feel her heart performing a very energetic dance and she was all at different temperatures. Where she had balanced on Jack's icy arm was a strange dead region as if that part of her body didn't exist at all.

'Sit,' said Jack and slopped Caleb's head back into the cauldron. He talked to Blossom over his shoulder in case she forgot herself again. 'Lud and all his court have hair of straw,' he said. 'What would he say, indeed, if he saw this boy with hair the colour of mud? How he is your brother I do not understand. Your hair has caught the light of the moon. There are few here with better.'

Blossom pretended her gold circlet needed adjusting, just so that she could touch her shiny hair, washed yesterday and no longer in its pony tail.

'Take the smaller cloth and when I turn his face upwards press the cloth tightly to it. I have used lime in the cauldron and if drops of it fall on his eyes, they will destroy them. What a blind worm he will be, here beneath the ground.'

Blossom thought the possibility of Caleb's being blinded by Jack's lime shampoo wasn't at all funny. She snatched the cloth and, when Jack, whose own hands couldn't be burnt it seemed, swung Caleb's head upwards so that his face was pointing towards the ceiling, she swooped down with her cloth, pressing much too firmly. Jack took another cloth, a not very absorbent sort of towel, and wrapped it around Caleb's dripping hair. Caleb then knocked Blossom away.

'I haven't got a rubber neck.'

'Go blind then!'

'Put on the garments,' said Jack who was suddenly no longer in the nondescript corduroys he always wore when he met the children above ground. He now had on grey trousers, boots with pointed toes and a grey tunic with jagged edges that reached almost to his knees. He looked like the true Jack Frost and yet he didn't.

As Caleb pulled on his own loose trousers, a shapeless woollen shirt and leather slippers, all the time trying not to disturb his turban, Blossom studied Jack's outfit. There was something wrong. It was the dark grey of thunderclouds. That was it. Jack wasn't the spirit who brought the rain; he was the king of frost and ice and he should have been in bright silver. His eyes and hair were lacklustre now too. As his power diminished, he was becoming greyer and darker - Blossom knew this was the truth. It was like looking at a harlequin who has lost all his glitter. Similar thoughts were going through Jack's mind.

'When you are ready, I shall take you into the palace. I am Jack without colour now. Soon I shall be dark as these walls of earth and no-one will know that I am there. Courtiers will hurry past me, rushing to the sun that will blaze forever, and they will not see me, Jack, a cold shadow.'

'It mustn't happen,' said Blossom who was beginning to feel very upset.

'You are two children who have it in your power to cloud the sun and bring us Winter.'

He turned back to Caleb, loosened the cloth on his head and vigorously dried his hair. Then he ran his fingers through it until it was all pointing stiffly backwards. It was now straw-coloured.

'Great!' said Caleb half able to see himself reflected in Blossom's brooch.

'Do not finger your hair, you curious, foolish boy. You will not wear the cloak, I think. You are not a princeling.'

Caleb looked upset. He wanted to swish around in a cloak like Blossom. You never saw a king without a cloak in pictures.

'You're not missing anything,' said Blossom. 'I want to scratch all over. I'm only wearing mine for the brooch.'

'You wear it because you are told,' corrected Jack. 'Now you will have food for you must be strong and not fade away as I am doing. There are cakes and drink'

As on their last visit, the table held a tray with a flagon and goblets and also a plate of little cakes.

'Children enjoy sweet things,' said Jack. 'I shall not eat, for it is not food I need to give me strength.'

Blossom wasn't going to be caught so easily. Jack might have nearly made her cry when he talked of going all dark or invisible, but he had also joked about Caleb's being a blind earthworm. He wasn't going to trap her by playing on her sympathy. He had tried to trick them into eating his underground food last time.

'Caleb, don't you ever learn?' she said sharply.

Caleb had been reaching out for one of the cakes. Admittedly, they looked delicious. He felt very silly. Fancy having your sister twice stop you from eating food that might trap you underground for ever.

'Do you promise it's not magic food that will make us stay here?' asked Blossom quite harshly.

Jack raised his eyebrows.

'We'll only eat them if you promise by everything most special to you that it's safe.'

Caleb thought she was being unbelievably brilliant.

Jack still didn't speak. He looked at the cakes and the flagon of drink and Blossom suspected he was taking a spell off them.

'I swear, as I hope to rescue Winter, that you may eat the cakes and partake of the drink and receive no harm,' said Jack eventually.

'That's not good enough,' said Blossom. 'If you kept us down here, you'd say it wasn't doing us any harm.'

Caleb thought it was time he butted in.

'We brought some sandwiches. They're in my duffle bag. There's Marmite and blackcurrant jam or salad cream and paste. You probably wouldn't like them.'

'Eat well,' said Jack. 'You must not lack vigour. Do you have drink?'

'Cokes and bananas,' said Blossom. 'We've got absolutely everything we need, thank you.'

They had their picnic then and there with Jack sitting on the fleeces, head in hands. He didn't speak a single word as they munched and chatted a little. Even the pop and hiss as they opened their cola cans didn't reach him. When they had finished eating, Caleb took the bread saw out of the duffle bag and slid it into the belt of his trousers. Then he made sure his shirt was very baggy over it. Blossom took her own secret weapon, which she had retrieved from the duffle bag without Caleb noticing, and concealed it in her cloak. It wasn't a secret weapon she could think of any way of using, but it was reassuring to have it all the same.

Caleb tugged Jack's sleeve. 'We're ready.'

Jack stood up almost before he had opened his eyes.

'The strength should be in your heart. A puny knife will not avail you,' he said.

Caleb reddened and Blossom tightened her grip on the silly object underneath her cloak.

'The palace awaits us. Come.'

He disappeared through the wall and it was only a moment before the children followed him. As they went to meet the greatest adventure of their lives, they found themselves holding hands tightly as if they were very little once more.

CHAPTER TEN

The Search Begins

They had been walking along one of the earthen corridors when Jack suddenly stopped.

'Here my magic ends.'

'You mean it's not safe from now on?' asked Caleb.

'I mean what I say. Your own strength and your own wisdom must guide you from this moment.'

Neither Caleb nor Blossom felt strong or wise. They felt like two people who have been tricked into doing something silly, like putting their hands into a beehive or jumping from the top board at a swimming pool when they can't dive or even swim.

'Why have you stopped?'

'I was just thinking...,' began Caleb but he didn't finish his sentence.

When you have rolled up your sleeve and the top of the beehive has been opened for you, it is very difficult to say, 'I don't think I'll bother after all.'

Controlling his impatience, Jack leant against the wall.

Blossom was sure she could feel the exact spot where Jack's magic protection ended. One moment you felt sort of comfortable and then you took a step and you immediately felt lost and worried and in an unfriendly place. She stepped back several paces pulling Caleb with her. Jack tapped his sharp nails on the wall and looked long and hard at the children.

'Don't worry,' said Caleb. 'We're getting ready. After three, Blossom. One…'

They counted very quickly and then rushed forward as if they had finally found the courage to leap into the pool.

Once they had started to trot, they felt they couldn't stop. To stop was to lose heart. They found themselves cantering and then galloping, hand in hand, down a succession of passages that constantly divided and turned at odd angles. They didn't hesitate once and Jack was always close behind them. With every stride he took, his grey clad knee and foot would just appear in the corner of Caleb's vision.

When the passage finally led them into a long, high room, even then the children didn't stop. They moved with the same fast steps across the room to the far wall where a line of narrow rectangular windows let in what appeared to be daylight. They sat down in one of the window recesses and looked at Jack, hoping he would tell them what to do next.

'Turn your heads,' he said, because they had been afraid to look out of the window at what lay beyond.

'You ran with sure steps. I did not need to guide you. Behold, Lud's kingdom.'

Blossom gasped. They were so high up.

'It's the Heath,' said Caleb.

'No, it is below the Heath.'

In front of the building in which they found themselves, and many, many feet below, was a landscape of grass and trees and flowers almost identical to the one they were used to playing in. The colours might have been a little brighter, that was all.

'But there's the sky,' said Blossom. 'It's whitey-blue.'

'No. The ceiling of our world is set with many jewels of the kind that you have seen. Their light blends and makes a kind of sky. When it is night in your world, these jewels fade and tinier, white jewels can then be seen which are our stars.'

'Do you have constellations?'

'No,' said Jack. 'We do not have your Orion the hunter or your monstrous bear. In that respect, your world is lovelier than ours. Our stars make no patterns. They are simply diamonds. There were times, long ago, when all our kind would freely wander your fields and look up at the sky and frame great questions. We do not feel wanted there now.'

'You can't just send us out there,' said Blossom in a small voice. 'We haven't got a map or anything.'

'Did you need a map when you outpaced me here?'

'That was different.'

'It was not different. If you but knew half the powers you have at your command. What you see from the window I shall name for you and then you must go down.'

'People are running about. They'll see us,' said Caleb.

'They exalt in the Summer. Misguided...' Jack suddenly broke off and gave no indication that he intended to say anything more. Caleb and Blossom who had been trying to work out exactly what the people below were engaged in doing, finally turned and stared at him. His face looked very sad. He didn't mind the children staring as first one tear and then many others trickled from his eyes. Blossom felt her own eyelashes go blurred too, though she was beginning to suspect Jack switched on his sadness when he wanted to win them over.

'I almost expected you to cry snowflakes,' she said.

'What good is this?' said Jack sharply pulling himself together. 'They say they want to play forever in the Summer sun. When I lay my sheet of frost and snow over your world, it is also white and chill here. Lud dons his cloak of fur and blows on his fingers. Great fires are lit, Samhain fires.'

He leant between the children and put his hand uncomfortably on Caleb's shoulder and pointed. 'One path leads from the palace door and circles the kingdom. If you follow it, you will soon come to the cliffs that are our borders. The other path leads to the centre of the kingdom, to

Brigantia's grove where stands the apple tree. It is an ancient grove, but dangerous.'

'If it's got lots of tall trees, I think I can see it in the distance,' said Blossom. She was determined not to be ignored, even though Jack had turned his back on her and was giving all his attention to Caleb.

'Beyond the grove are such hills as we can manage here and beyond them lie the waters.'

'*The waters*?'

'Two of the streams from your world dip into this kingdom for some of their length. They form little cascades which we like to sit and watch. After they have watered our fields, they re-emerge into the air and, as a single stream, flow down to the great river.'

'The Thames.'

'Yes,' said Jack not at all impressed by Caleb's quickness. 'But what none of you knows is that there is another, deeper, wider, more frightful stream that skirts a mere corner of our world and then plunges deep into the heart of the Earth. Lud himself would not bathe in the dark pool which is all we see of this stream.'

'Gosh.'

'If you plunge into that water, do not call my name. There are things here which even gods cannot control. That is all I should say to you. Come.'

'*All*!' shouted the children together.

'We don't know how to behave,' said Caleb.

'Shall I have to curtsey?' asked Blossom.

'The less I tell you, the better. What you need to say or do, you will know when the time comes. If I give you instructions, that may confuse you. Trust yourselves.'

'I haven't got the slightest idea about anything,' said Blossom.

'All I shall say further is this,' said Jack. 'You, Blossom, are to find the whereabouts of the silver hand of Lud which

Brigantia has hidden. You, Caleb, are to find the apple of Brigantia. And both before Samhain. At all costs, before Samhain. Speak little, but listen constantly. Stand at the rear of gatherings and do not draw attention to yourselves. The king and queen can rage as you will never hear humans rage. Do not cross them. Obey them instantly. And never frown. I am afraid to cloud your judgement with too much knowledge, but I think I may say to you, Blossom, beware of Brigantia's three forms. No, you must not ask me to explain. Trust yourself and you will learn what I mean. Remember - her three forms. Address them as Great King and Great Queen. I shall say no more.'

'No more!'

'No more. Only in the sorest need must you call me. I shall help you if I can.'

'*If*,' thought Blossom with disgust. 'If. If. If. What if he *can't* help us? We might be put in prison or sacrificed. We don't even know if they speak English. Caleb will be all right if they speak in Latin because he's good at it. But I won't!'

She began to shiver.

Jack led them to one end of the room and stopped by a hole in the floor. He pointed to a rough stone staircase and simply said, 'Blossom.'

With more courage than she had ever thought she possessed, Blossom set her gold circlet straight, gave a little cough, lifted up the hem of her long dress and walked down the steps. She didn't look at Caleb nor say goodbye to him in case she gave way.

Part of her was still visible when Jack took Caleb firmly by the arm and marched him to the other end of the room.

'This is Lud's half of the palace. He and Brigantia never meet now, and, if their retainers pass each other, they wrangle.'

He pointed down a second staircase which fell away from a similar hole in the floor. There was no *Farewell*, nor *Good*

Luck, nor a friendly tap on the shoulder to signify that he was grateful for what the children were doing. In fact, he stalked away almost as soon as Caleb had put his foot on the first step.

'Bloss...!' shouted Caleb before he could stop himself. He disappeared from view with the great dusty room echoing half his sister's name.

CHAPTER ELEVEN

Blossom

Blossom descended through two or three empty floors before objects began to appear - wooden chests, bales of cloth, pyramids of dishes. Still down, and finally she heard voices. They were voices of young girls and it was obvious to Blossom that she was bound to make hundreds of friends her own age, all of them full of admiration for her princess-looks and the way her hair slid from beneath her circlet like golden rain.

She walked away from the staircase and had been standing watching their agitated backs for some minutes before they noticed her. There was time for her to see that they wouldn't fall in admiration at her feet after all. How could you expect girls dressed in silk to be impressed by one in wool? Jack, whose cruel idea of a joke it must be, had turned her out like a serving girl. This thought made it no surprise when one of the girls stood up from the large chest in which she and her companions were searching and said, 'She's standing there. How dare she!'

'I had a pain,' said Blossom sharply.

'Palace servants don't have pains. Which one did she tell us to fetch?'

The trio of girls started to talk all at once again and then to shout and wave their arms. They clearly couldn't agree over a matter of some importance. Blossom walked over and looked into the chest. Its contents reminded her of the P.E.

box at Primary School - skipping ropes, hoops and balls, but these were delicate creations of gold and silver.

'What did she mean? What did she mean?' shrieked and moaned the girls. 'We can't take the wrong ball. She's in one of her punishing moods this morning.'

'What did she say exactly?' asked Blossom.'

'You heard the queen , you deaf door-post. She said, *Bring me my favourite throwing ball*. And we don't know which one she meant.'

Blossom's eyes roved over the inside of the chest. What did the queen want with metal throwing balls? Did *she* amuse herself by throwing them at people and knocking their heads off? Jack had told her to be confident, so she reached her hand into the chest and said, 'The Great Queen likes this one best.'

It was a golden ball, obviously hollow and exceedingly light. The decoration on the top of it reminded Blossom of the leaves and stalks of an apple. It was an appropriate ball in view of what she and Caleb were supposed to be searching for.

'The apple one.' 'Perhaps she meant that one.' 'You shouldn't have touched it, you're not a handmaiden.' 'Do you think she'll be able to tell that a serving girl touched it?' 'Come on, the queens's waiting. We'll have to go.'

They ran to the top of the staircase.

'What are you standing there for?' demanded one girl as Blossom made no attempt to follow.

'It's my pain again.'

'Go downstairs at once.'

The girls stood aside to let her through. The bossiest gave her hair a hard pull as she passed by, but Blossom took this as a kind of compliment. She hurried down the staircase which was now wider and more impressive, the rough steps giving way to ones covered with a polished red wood on which her feet slipped from time to time. The girls were behind her prodding her on.

In the room below, she found more handmaidens running about and waving.

'Take this,' said a voice as a rug-length roll of silk suddenly bent itself over Blossom's shoulders. 'Well get outside. They look as if they're going to beat us today,' and a hand or foot was applied to her back.

As the girls carrying objects were all exiting through the same door, Blossom went that way too. She found herself in a hallway and then outside. Girls dressed in both wool and silk were throwing objects onto the grass and then rushing inside for more.

'Perhaps there's a fire,' thought Blossom, in which case she wasn't going back.

She carried her roll of silk to the far side of the heap and dropped it onto the ground. And there she stayed. She knelt down and examined the silk closely, pretending to look for tears or loose threads.

'Don't cuddle it, unroll it,' said a bossy voice.

Blossom therefore unrolled the silk which was grass green and covered with a design of interwoven paler leaves and red and yellow flowers. Other girls were busy smoothing down other rolls of silk and so she concentrated on flattening out the creases, hoping no-one would take any notice of her or tread on her. The piles of objects were making more sense. Fifteen or twenty thin sheets of silk had been spread on the grass, their colours and serpentining patterns overlapping dizzily. A mountainous semi-circle of cushions rose up all of a sudden and Blossom retreated as she was sure that something important was going to happen on or near them and she didn't want to be caught right in the middle of it. She continued to grovel, patting and smoothing and muttering phrases like, 'The grass keeps pushing up this corner.' Some way away, in front of another door to the palace, she could see a crowd of boys engaged in the same kind of activity as the girls. They were equally urgent.

'Then the whisper went round, 'Here she comes. I hope we're in time.'

Blossom couldn't help looking up at this moment as Queen Brigantia came out of the palace in state. She was beautiful and terrifying at the same time. Her hair was red and stood out wildly from her head in points and scoops. Lost somewhere in amongst it was a small crown. Her dress and cloak were of such light silk it wouldn't have been surprising if they had turned into little clouds and floated away from her. The cloak was silver and covered with interwoven flowers and leaves the red and green of her hair and dress. It seemed to need the gaggle of attendants not so much to hold it off the ground as to hold it down. On the queen's arms were spirals of gold and her fingers were heavy with rings. Around her neck she had a fine twisted collar of gold which ended in two birds' heads. The collar emphasised what was for Blossom the most embarrassing feature of Brigantia's appearance - at the front she was naked to the waist, and nobody seemed to find this unusual in a member of the royal family.

The queen advanced a few steps and then waved her arms triumphantly, pointing to the crowd of boys.

'You're first out today, girls. That's cheered me up no end,' she said in a voice that Blossom felt was unlikely ever to be used gently.

'Lud will skulk inside the palace and rant and rave and make everyone's life a misery. Good. He can stay there peeping from behind the curtains until we choose to go away. All wave to him, girls. Now!'

The girls vigorously waved towards the windows of the palace nearest the other entrance. Blossom's wave, however, was tiny as it seemed a babyish thing to be doing, but she didn't go un-noticed.

'Little Miss Woollen Dress doesn't have much energy for waving. Perhaps she didn't like my suggestion.'

'I had a pain,' said Blossom uninventively.

A nearby girl winced. Blossom had answered back.

Brigantia was surprised that words had been returned when, for hundreds of years, there had been polite silence. 'I thought I wouldn't have to lose my temper for at least half an hour,' she said. 'But I'm going to be proved wrong, aren't I? By someone who's dropped out of a kitchen cupboard, too. Well, now she can wave to the king all on her own and let's hope he remembers her face. Move aside, girls, so he can get a clear view of her. Perhaps he'll turn her into stone. Or perhaps I will.'

When the queen was satisfied that Blossom had skipped up and down and waved sufficiently, she signalled for her to stop.

'I'll forgive you this time because of your hair, but pretty hair doesn't mean you're free to speak when you haven't been invited to.'

She wound a length of Blossom's hair around her white finger and soon had enough to give it a very painful pull if she chose.

'Does it, little one?'

There was the beginning of a tug, but this time Blossom realised she was meant to reply.

'Oh no, Great Queen. Forgive me. Forgive me.'

She fell on her knees because she thought it was the right thing to do and because she was sure those piercing green eyes were capable of reading all Jack's secrets in her face. The queen didn't let go of her hair as she fell to the ground, so there was a jerk that made her eyes water.

'Little fool,' said Brigantia and finally decided to lie on the cushions.

Breakfast, in the form of cakes, slices of fruit and coloured drinks in goblets, was brought in and set before the queen on low stools. She overturned several plates and dishes before she found the food that exactly suited her taste buds that morning. When she had finished eating and had had her hair brushed into new peaks and her fingers rinsed in scented water, she announced, 'Now for the games. Have you brought my favourite ball to play with?'

'We have, O Queen.'

The ball decorated like an apple was held out for her inspection.

'Who has been bribed by the king to play this trick on me?' she asked all in one cold breath.

It was an unfounded accusation but no-one dared say so. In the silence, the queen's anger went from icy to lava-hot and she dug her fingers deeply into the cushions beside her. Her eyes roved over the dumb gathering of attendants and it didn't take her long to spot that Blossom looked more frightened than the rest. Brigantia beckoned and Blossom stumbled forward.

'Was this your idea?'

'Yes, Great Queen, I ...'

'Knowing I have lost the apple from my tree?'

'Yes, Great Queen, I...'

'You present me with this mockery of it?'

'Yes, Great Queen, I...'

Jack, that unreliable friend, had said, 'Trust yourselves and do not ask for guidance.' He had insisted that they would know exactly what to do and say as each situation arose and here she was having done and said entirely the wrong thing and having lightning and volcanoes thrown at her.

'Because I threw his cold old silver hand away, he bribed you with some nick-nack and told you to annoy me.'

'No, Great Queen. I...I...I've brought you a present,' almost shouted Blossom who thought she ought to come up with anything to divert the queen's attention before it was too late.

'A present!'

Brigantia's voice dropped at once from shrieking level to the gentle cooing of an iron dove.

Blossom took her secret weapon from under her cloak. All this time she had managed to cling to it. If it didn't work, she was convinced she would end up as little charred pieces scattered over a wide area. She hoped Caleb would manage to take one or two of them home, unless he ended up as little charred pieces too.

'What kind of present is it? Is it extremely valuable?'

Blossom opened the pink, heart-shaped object and displayed it to the queen.

'It used to belong to a beautiful princess up there in the human world. It's a manicure set. Very extremely valuable.'

When she had told Caleb she had a weapon she could use to fight off enemies, she had meant the nail scissors, or, at a pinch, the tweezers.

'Well?' said the queen.

'Let me show you.'

'What do you intend to do?'

'I need a bowl of warm water you can soak your fingers in.'

She wondered how she could be so brave, standing there making suggestions to the queen as if they had known each other for years. 'Perhaps,' she thought, 'I've gone mad or I'm already dead.'

'Fetch her all she asks for,' ordered Brigantia enjoying the buzz of distress from her handmaidens who were shocked and jealous of the attention being paid to a serving girl.

'Sit by me in the meantime and let me look at you.'

Blossom sat on a cushion as far away as she dared and silently urged the girls to hurry with the water.

'I said let me look at you. Don't stare at the ground!'

Blossom raised her head and tried to look past Brigantia rather than at those knowledgeable eyes.

'My eyes are in the middle of my face, not in a ring round it, so far as I know. You're doing your best to put me in a temper again aren't you?'

Blossom was desperate, but at last the water was brought out with as much ceremony as frantic haste would allow. Her first instinct was to pick up the queen's hand and splash it down into the water. Her fingers were almost around Brigantia's wrist before she decided this might not be such a good idea. Perhaps the queen was allowing her hundreds of yards of rope to hang herself.

'Would you please put your hand in the water, o great queen.'

Brigantia obliged and Blossom felt the eyes of everyone move from the bowl back to herself to see what she did next.

'We have to wait for your cuticles to soften.'

'I can't wait. Deal with my hand now.'

Brigantia withdrew her hand from the water and held it out for Blossom's attention. Blossom dried it very carefully, trying with all her concentration not to squeeze it in case Brigantia said, 'That hurts!' and made her disappear. The really dangerous part was yet to come, however. Brigantia's hand hadn't soaked long enough to make the cuticles soft and manageable. Mrs Belling-Peake told Blossom to put Fairy Liquid in the water to help the softening process, but she could hardly ask for washing up liquid, even though all the liquids down there were fairy ones. What if the little tool gouged holes in the base of Brigantia's nails or Blossom's hand slipped and she ploughed a deep scratch as far back as the knuckle?

'Don't shake,' Blossom told herself. 'You'll end up with bits of skin all over the place.'

She turned the queen's fingers at an angle and applied an emery board to the side of a nail. Brigantia seemed to be tensing because her hand, which had felt soft, was now harder and, before her eyes, Blossom saw the nail thicken, yellow and grow more pointed. It looked like the discoloured paring from a cow's horn. She continued to stare at the queen's hand, but, out of the corner of her eye, she saw the hems of the girls' skirts move backwards. Something could be about to happen. Forcing herself, and it was very difficult, Blossom let her eyes range up the queen's arm. It was thinner and an armlet of gold had slid down to the wrist. Veins had appeared too. Blossom's gaze continued upwards, past the short sleeve of the dress and across. The smooth neck had grown folds and the white breasts she had been shy to look at were inches lower and pointed, ending in long brown nipples like the ones you see on animals. By the second, Brigantia's skin puckered and came more to resemble a piece of cloth that needed ironing.

'Look at me, sweet child,' said the queen in a new voice.

She gave a brief, shrill laugh and Blossom saw a drapery of loose throat skin shake. When her eyes reached Brigantia's chin, she hoped wildly that she would faint. There was a deep, off-centre cleft in the chin and knots of bristles had sprouted here and there. All the new features reminded her of animals, the eagle claws, the turkey neck, the pig bristles and the pig other things. She moved up to the thin, cracked lips with the odd brown tooth pressing over them. The nose had developed a bony ridge and sank in for two thirds of its length, although it bubbled out at its tip and was freely sprinkled with blackheads. The whole face was framed by greasy hanks of hair with the occasional streak of pale red. The eyes were worst of all. Both were still green, but there was a web of red blood vessels in the white of the right one which also oozed and a thick drop of sticky inflammation hung on the lower lashes.

Brigantia, very pleased with herself, moved her head from side to side so that she could take in Blossom's pale look of horror from several angles. There was a kind of croaking in her throat and when she exhaled her breath smelt.

Blossom could feel herself toppling backwards and very soon the stool with the dish of water on had been overturned and she was lying looking up through blurring eyes at Brigantia's brown smile.

CHAPTER TWELVE

Games But No Fun

'You see. *I* can do silly things too,' said Brigantia. 'Now get up.'

In an instant she had returned to her former self. Blossom didn't dare permit herself the luxury of pretended unconsciousness and she stumbled to her feet. Her legs weren't entirely under her control, however, and she lurched in all directions as she tried to join the party of serving girls who had come out of the palace. The cushions and silk carpets were to be carried to a grassy hollow a little way away, a small natural theatre, where prying eyes from the palace would have difficulty seeing them. The queen had begun the morning as she had begun all her mornings recently, by trying to make sure that she got out of the palace first and bagged the spot in front of it for her breakfast table before Lud did. And now it was time to play. Blossom had noticed that breakfast-time for Brigantia and Lud meant nearly noon.

'Forward girls,' said Brigantia. 'Let the misery enjoy his late breakfast in peace. Kigva, you can carry the present Little Miss Yellow Hair gave me. It's horrible but I might find a use for it sometime. Walk behind me, not in front. Who do you think you are!'

Kigva slipped back half a dozen paces, turning her head as she did so to look for Blossom who was bringing up the rear with the other heavily-laden serving girls. When their eyes met, Blossom didn't need a dictionary to translate the look on

Kigva's face. It clearly shouted, 'I am your enemy.'

Blossom tripped at once. No-one could have let Jack down more than she was doing. You simply couldn't afford to have enemies when you were in a foreign country and trying to find a magic apple and a silver hand in less than a week.

Kigva tossed her head and turned away again. It might just have been a twitch of her nose and a slip of her foot that followed, but Blossom, who could still see the girl's face in profile, was sure that she had pulled a face behind Brigantia's back and then done a saucy wiggle. One or two girls drew in their breath sharply as if to confirm this. Brigantia strode on, apparently oblivious of the small rebellion behind her, and chose the spot where she wished to recline.

The handmaidens played the games and the serving girls fanned them and gave them drinks in exchange for pinches and scolding. Brigantia had divided her train into teams and she made all the decisions when it wasn't clear who had won a particular skipping or catching game. Blossom was one of those deputed to hold the end of the skipping rope for *The ravens in the tree are one, two, three* and, although she prided herself on her skill when swinging a rope, her timing kept going wrong and girl after girl was hit on the head or nose or bottom with the rope or simply fell over with it knotted around her ankles.

'I didn't mean it,' apologised Blossom the first time and was promptly told to hush.

She was afraid she would turn all the girls against her in the space of minutes, but, strangely, none of them looked at her resentfully. At least one was fighting back tears.

'So why don't they hate me too?' Blossom asked herself.

'That *was* fun, wasn't it?' said Brigantia. 'You never get that game right even though I've promised a beautiful brooch to anyone whose jackdaw, or whatever it is, in the tree counts to a hundred and one, two, three.'

So there was the explanation. Magic. It was silly to expect a queen not to cheat. The bigger you are, the more effectively you can cheat.

'Now for the best game, the one with the ball my handmaidens let a scullery urchin choose for me.'

The girls who had been run off their feet in pursuit of Brigantia's fun knew they were in for more exhausting exercise. It was a kind of *Pig-in-the-middle* game and Brigantia made them play it and play it. Kigva was skilful and cunning in the way she threw the ball so that it was just beyond the reach of the poor, isolated *pig*, and she was rarely called on to go into the centre of the circle herself. Blossom stood with the other serving girls ready to supply refreshments when one of the participants was allowed a brief rest. If the ball were thrown too hard and landed near them, they were permitted to throw it back, but not to take part in the game.

When the ball landed exactly between Blossom's feet, Brigantia said, 'It obviously wants you in the game. Shall we let her play? I said: **Shall we let her play**?'

'Yes, yes O Great Queen.' 'What fun.' 'Hooray!'

It was one of the few occasions when Kigva was *pig* which perhaps meant that the queen had eyes in the back of her head after all and that no funny face and saucy wiggle ever went unobserved.

'Whoever can keep the ball away from Kigva the best can have this revolting pink gift. If Kigva catches the ball quickly, *she* has the gift. What could be fairer?'

The voice of safety told Blossom to throw the ball gently and accurately into Kigva's hand, but it was the voice of madness she obeyed when she threw it high over Kigva's head. It was *her* manicure set after all.

A second girl, anxious to please, did throw the ball too obviously to Kigva.

'I wouldn't do that, if I were you,' said Brigantia quietly. 'Start again. That go doesn't count.'

The ball landed in Blossom's hand on two occasions out of three and she found herself lobbing it brilliantly over the *pig's* head and feigning one way and then throwing it another, even with spin on it as if she were one of those cricketers Caleb used to go on about.

The *pig* couldn't have had many genuine friends because, well before she sank into a tearful heap on the grass, it was obvious that three-quarters of the handmaidens were enjoying her come-uppance quite as much as Blossom.

'Stop that at once,' said Brigantia when the *pig's* sobs became more and more broken. 'And if you go whining to your mother, you'll know about it. Playtime's over. It's rest time now. Some can pick me flowers and make chains. Lots of the rest of you can fan me. Before you get too excited about the gift, Yellow Hair, I've decided to keep it for the time being.'

Having seen the size of the fans that had been brought along to keep Brigantia cool, Blossom decided it was a much more attractive job picking flowers. She scampered off and had quickly made a crown and a bracelet of unseasonal flowers - violets, buttercups and daisies. It wasn't clear what she was supposed to do with the flowers, so she hung back and watched. Kigva was sulking as much as she dared in public and trying to make her eyes less red by splashing water on them. Blossom offered her the bracelet of flowers and said, 'Can't we be friends?'

'Friends! With something from the kitchen!'

Buttercup, daisy and violet heads flew all over the place.

'My mother is Epona.'

'See if I care,' said Blossom.

'You *will* care.'

Blossom wandered off and placed her flowers with the rest around the cushion that was serving Brigantia as a pillow. A canopy of thin curtains was erected over the queen's head and upper body to keep the light from her eyes, but she was resting rather than sleeping because commands and reprimands were snapped from underneath the canopy at frequent intervals.

The girls with fans were supposed to usher gentle breezes into the open front of the canopy, but one had been too vigorous.

'If I wanted a Winter storm, I could ask that fool Jack Frost for one,' said the queen. 'I wonder what's become of him. Probably melted by now. To think we ever took him seriously. Did *you* ever take him seriously?'

'Oh no, Great Queen, never.'

'Yes you did. Don't tell lies. Hold that fan higher, you're not a windmill.'

Girls lay about the queen, talking in whispers or combing each other's hair, ever ready to spring to their feet if a command came.

'We need some music now,' said Brigantia. 'Something to celebrate Summer and Summer and Summer. Kigva, I want a forever-Summer song.'

Kigva found a small purse amongst the litter of objects they had carried from the palace and she took two small bells out of it. She held one in each hand and, finding a seat by the queen's feet, began to sing. There were no words to the song; it was merely a vocalise accompanied every now and again by chimes from the bells which were tuned to different notes. Kigva's singing made Blossom want to drift like a cloud or a leaf on an easy stream. When the song finished, she had drifted so far into her fleecy thoughts that she was at first unaware of the silence. And then she clapped. There are few moments worse than finding yourself the only person clapping at the wrong place in a concert. Clapping near a queen who is set on sleep is such a moment.

The royal legs, which protruded from the canopy, underwent a spasm and Blossom realised she had added one more item to her black list. As Kigva hurriedly began another soothing melody, a hand grasped Blossom by the shoulder.

'Come away.'

The serving girls quietly gathered armfuls of boxes, bags and games apparatus and tiptoed in the direction of the palace, leaving Brigantia in the care of the maids of honour. More voices joined in the song and the queen gave a deep, contented sigh.

Blossom left with great relief. Her head was buzzing with the effort of trying hard to be good and, at the same time, being terrified of punishment because she had failed. What if Brigantia had asked them all to sing. The only songs she knew the words of right through were *Nellie the Elephant* and *Sweet Phyllis Goes A-Maying* which they had been practising for two weeks in the music lessons and in which she still sang flat.

'I'm Enid,' said the girl who had led her away.

'I'm Blossom.'

'Everyone *must* know everyone else here. Is she going to ask me where I come from?' Blossom wondered.

'Why did you go against Kigva?'

'She's horrible.'

'She's allowed to be. Epona's her mother and *she's* got a temper worse than the queen's. As you know.'

'She knows I don't know. Can I trust her?' thought Blossom. 'I'll have to try harder in future,' she said.

'You can help me.'

Enid led her up an out-of-the-way staircase and along a passageway on the second floor. At the end was a great door which she unlocked.

'Don't do anything wrong here. Don't spill a drop of water, leave a grain of dust or forget a dead petal.'

It was the queen's bedroom with a large silk-hung red wood bed in its centre. Silk hangings embroidered with pictures of summer landscapes hung on the walls and all around the edges of the room were lightly-scented wooden chests.

They took sheets and pillow cases from one of the chests and changed the bed and afterwards they spread the fine coverlet creaselessly so that exactly the same quantity of it hung at each corner by the bedposts. Enid placed a dish of marigolds on the low table by the bed-head and said, 'These flowers so late in the year. She can't have enough of them.'

Looking at the bed with its light, high mattress, and the simple dish of marigolds that could easily have held strawberries or breakfast cereal, Blossom realised how tired she was and hungry. She wondered whether serving girls ate lunch down there and, if so, could she have hers immediately. She longed for chicken and roast potatoes and thick banana custard. It must have been well after three.

'Isn't it time to eat?' she ventured.

They found a clutch of serving girls in the process of leaving the kitchen armed with a meal for their mistress Epona. An oppressive smell of cooked liver or a coarse meat in broth hung in the air and you couldn't help but take in wet, unpleasant sniffs of it when you breathed. It was like being caught in a gravy cloud.

Enid took bread, cheese, apples and cakes from the cupboards and threw them into a basket. She gave Blossom a jug of milk to carry and bustled her out.

'It's always the same when Epona wants a meal with plenty of blood in, isn't it?' said Enid. ' The rest of us can never bear to stay in the kitchen.'

They climbed another half-hidden staircase and eventually found themselves in Enid's room. It had a small bed, a chest and a stool, but no carpets, hangings or fleeces and only the smallest of windows that let in a sort of twilight.

'I can't see to put the jug down,' said Blossom. 'I don't want to pour it all over your bed.'

'Wait.'

There was the sound of a chest lid being raised and the room was suddenly lit with a lilac radiance. Enid had placed a glowing stone on the chest top and Blossom did her usual trick of looking at one object while not paying attention to another she had in her hand. As the milk lapped to the rim of the jug and was about to splash onto the floor, Enid relieved Blossom of it and gently pushed her onto the bed.

'Just eat.'

Blossom did so, eagerly and gratefully, and when Enid said, 'Why not sleep a little?' she was happy to do that too.

When she awoke, the lilac stone had been replaced by a smaller blue one, a nightlight, and the square of window was entirely black. She had slept for hours and darkness had fallen on the worlds above and below the Heath. There would be dark, hot nights for ever if she and Caleb failed in the task Jack had set them. This worry slept when she did, but now it clutched at her again. 'Won't any old apple do?' she wondered. 'Couldn't we trick Jack with a golden delicious from the shop?'

CHAPTER THIRTEEN

Caleb

At first, Caleb met with fewer problems than Blossom. This was generally the case. People took to him, found him cute on occasion, whereas Blossom they eventually found tiresome as she tried too hard to be Little Miss Popular.

Like his sister, Caleb was quickly caught up in the early morning race to be first out of the palace. Squabbles amongst Lud's boys and amongst the men who gave them orders as to who exactly had the authority to give orders, meant that organisation of the male side of the palace was very poor. Benches would be half out of a door when a man's voice would demand, 'Who told you to carry that bench out? Who? Well, take it back until *I* say you can take it out.'

The boys ran round and round and up and down to little purpose and there was very little of Lud's household clutter outside when Brigantia made her triumphant debut. Caleb was cuffed and kicked harder almost than he could bear, but, as this was happening to all the other boys and as none of it was aimed at him personally, he just about managed to take it in his stride.

He could see the girls with their silks and cushions, but he didn't spot Blossom until she was made to wave entirely on her own. His heart all but reached his mouth when he saw her. She looked very alone and vulnerable, but there was nothing he dared say against the scowlings and mutterings when the king's retinue felt the shame of the queen's humiliation of them yet again.

Lud strode angrily back and forth in one of the downstairs rooms, never once looking out of the window after the golden-haired child had pranced her derision at him. He was a tall man with eyes too blue to look into and bleached hair swept back from his temples and raggedly down his neck as if he had faced into a storm. A huge, white walrus moustache overhung his mouth. A heavy gold torch at least two inches in diameter and with silver inlaid circles at its end, rested on his thick shoulders. He was dressed in the loose linen trousers that all his court wore, the only difference being that his jewellery - his rings and armlets and his dagger hilt - were bigger and more encrusted with red garnets and enamels.

Caleb peeped from a great distance at this impressive creature and wondered how on earth he was going to find out what the king had done with Brigantia's apple. If he asked outright, he expected that he would be snapped in half.

When Brigantia and her train withdrew for their games, Lud's men were outside in a flash. The king's last words before he began his silent prowling around the room had been, 'If this ever happens again.' It had been a mighty *If* and the unfinished sentence, with its suggestion of the worst punishments imaginable, had added wings to their heels.

The king's high-backed wooden chair, of that red wood again and softened with fat cushions, was placed on the grass and then men sat on benches at his feet with the boys squatting on the grass behind them.

The king's breakfast was cold meat, bread and wine, which he ate vigorously and noisily, spluttering wine-soggy fragments all around him as he laughed and shouted. His ill-humour had subsided with his first cups of wine. When he had progressed a long way with his breakfast, the men were served theirs by the boys. Caleb quickly saw what was required and set to serving the meal in exactly the same way as all the other boys were doing. His good luck failed him at this point as he surreptitiously picked a slither of cold beef from a plate he was carrying. He was seen doing this and was punished by having the plate banged up into his face by the man whose breakfast it was intended to be. Caleb was hardly aware of what had happened to him, except that his feet were off the ground and his nose was so painful it must be bleeding.

'Keep your brat's hands out of my breakfast,' he heard as he continued his arc through the air and landed at the king's feet. Lud kicked him away.

'Arawn chooses his adversaries well,' said a second man's voice, chuckling. 'Such a mighty fist for such a puny warrior.'

This brought an appreciative tremor of laughter from the other men and further enraged Arawn into whose breakfast Caleb had so unwisely stuck his fingers.

'Where is he!' said the angry man as the *he* in question, sensing what was coming, hid behind the king's chair. The chase which then took place made Arawn look more foolish and therefore feel more angry. Caleb dodged amongst the company and hopped over benches, but, thankfully, no-one made any attempt to hold him as they all found it so entertaining. Disaster seemed in sight, however, as Caleb, at one end of a passage between two benches, saw Arawn bearing down on him from the other end. A heavy metal plate found its way into his hand and, automatically, he skimmed it at Arawn's head. He was very good at this as Mr Belling-Peake had spent hours on the Heath with his son practising with the family frisbee. Caleb half dreaded and half hoped to see the top of his attacker's head sliced off like a boiled egg, but Arawn had been in too many skirmishes and he ducked in time.

'Enough,' said the king, barring Arawn's way with his arm. 'You think *your* honour has been marked by this child. What of *my* honour? Are you to overturn the tables at my every meal? The boy was at fault and, in my eyes, you are even more at fault. But to each of us reparation must be paid.'

'I beg your pardon Great King.'

'I accept that. Come here, boy,' said Lud.

Caleb moved forwards, wondering whether he was going to be accused of attempted murder.

'He bleeds from the nose, you see,' said the king. 'That is the recompense he makes you as a warrior. But I shall be his surety. For every drop of blood there on his front, I shall give you a gemstone and let me see the lips of none here crease in laughter. It is over.'

Arawn set about ordering boys to repair the disorder he had caused.

'You need not work,' Lud said to Caleb. 'Sit at my feet for the present. Though Arawn could hold you in his fist, you withstood him. Where should we have hung his head, I wonder, if you had struck it from his shoulders with the plate?'

He motioned towards the doorway of the palace which Caleb paid attention to for the first time. The lintels had a succession of niches in them, most containing a carved stone head. The heads were identical. They had pointed chins, tiny mouths and slits for eyes. The niches that were still empty worried Caleb.

'I am amused by the notion of Arawn's head on a plate,' said Lud. 'I am casting my mind back to old foes and old battlefields. All I have to fight with now is my queen. Lud the mighty stealing an apple.'

He drew his left arm from under his cloak and looked sadly at the wrist which ended in neither a silver hand nor a real one.

'We shall be warriors today.'

Caleb hoped he wouldn't be expected to take part.

'You have grown fat in these high days of Summer,' announced the king. ' I want you all lean again as when the island of Logris above us was ours.'

He ordered Arawn and various of the senior men to accompany him as he walked to the spot he had chosen for their war games. The rest were to see to the collecting of javelins, swords, shields and drink from the palace.

'The little warrior with the plate shall walk beside me as he has made me smile,' said Lud. 'What kin are you of, boy?'

'I haven't got any kin, Great King,' replied Caleb feeling as alone as the remark made him sound.

'No kin! Then I shall foster you. You will grow up to be the king's own man.'

His thick fingers pinched Caleb's arm to feel how much muscle there was.

'That will be after many Summers. Your limbs are light as a bird's. Would you fly if I told you to?'

'I'd have a go.'

'So you would try to be a sparrow for your king. Perhaps you will be a hawk in time. Take up the plate you showed such skill with. I shall give a dagger to the boy who can pitch it farthest. Today I shall give gifts. We have Summer days without end to throw and tussle in.'

They walked for about a quarter of a mile away from the palace, Caleb at the king's side with the gold plate under his arm. One boundary of the kingdom was soon reached. They came to the cliffs that Jack had mentioned and walked along their foot for a while. The palace, from that distance, was a whitish wall with higgledy-piggledy windows rising many storeys between the fringeing cliffs like a Tibetan monastery. The kingdom fanned out in front of the palace. It was as if a whole country had been reduced to a miniature. There were low hills or mounds for mountains, groups of a dozen trees for forests and, for rivers, there were streams you could step over without increasing your stride. Lud and his companions did, in fact, need to cross one of the large streams that Jack had said meandered through the kingdom before bursting into the outside world, but even this was accomplished by means of half a dozen stepping stones.

It was a wonderful day as far as Caleb was concerned. He revelled in the thump as wrestling bodies hit the ground or the gasps and applause as one of the javelins, and real battle-tested javelins they were, soared farther than the rest. The winners looked triumphant and the losers took their defeats bitterly. Caleb didn't win the throwing the plate competition as his skill with a frisbee was cancelled out by the sheer muscle power of some of the boys. He expected Lud to be angry with him because his newly chosen attendant had come so nearly last, but the king was philosophical about it and pointed to the wine flagon again.

The excitement gradually died away as men and boys became hoarse from cheering, exhausted from competing and more and more tipsy. They snoozed and chatted and had their bruises rubbed. It was a very welcome hour or two of calm after so much flinging about.

Finally Lud announced that he was returning to the palace.

'Prepare a good feast tonight,' he said. 'All this has not made me as light as I thought. You, young cub,' to Caleb, 'will bring me my meat at the feasting. I demand good service. Beware.'

He flicked the end of his cloak around his left arm to hide the lack of a hand and stumbled off quietly and miserably, not as you would normally expect a king to exit, to a fanfare and with splendour.

Although Caleb would have liked to examine the weapons closely as they were stacked in the chariot again, some of the swords had accidentally drawn blood and were sticky with it, he knew such curiosity would look suspicious. So he made himself useful and kept as far away as possible from Arawn who had easily won the wrestling.

In the palace, the boys were left to put the weapons neatly away in an armoury that made Caleb wide-eyed. Swords and javelins extended along three walls like fish bones and the figure-of-eight shields were giant, dully-gleaming leaves on the other. Afterwards, the boys threw themselves down on the fleeces of a large dormitory and Caleb, glad of the peace and quiet, found the most remote corner where he could be alone with his thoughts. These mostly concerned the silver hand that was at the heart of Jack's plan. You simply didn't come across silver hands by accident. They didn't lie on shelves or under cushions calling out for you to spot them. He and Blossom would never succeed and Jack had made what followed their failure seem so terrible. Caleb dug his fingers into his palms and almost cried. It wasn't fair to ask so much of them.

CHAPTER FOURTEEN

A Feast

The early flames finally took hold of the log and began to char its sides. The fire dogs, like large, fully-opened pairs of scissors, supported the log at either end, keeping it high enough from the ground to allow the flames full play.

The flames from other burning logs made a circle of light in the darkness of the night beneath the Heath. A cauldron of vegetables was stewing over one fire and a haunch of beef was being slowly turned by Caleb over another. From time to time, globblet of fat dropped from the meat and, if they missed the trough meant to catch them, hissed and flared when they met the flames. Caleb had been given a beaker and told to dip it occasionally into the trough of fat and to baste the beef with it. He was left alone because it was smelly and sweaty work on such a warm night.

The king wouldn't appear until the feast was prepared and the newly-lit log was to be his. It was not strictly necessary, and he would probably soon be sweating as much as Caleb, but no feast was considered complete without flames dancing nearby.

The best plates and drinking vessels were brought out: a gold drinking horn for the king with a ram's head emerging from the coils of its narrow end, and any number of wine flagons whose red and yellow enamels caught the light.

Caleb noticed more and more figures moving around the edge of the light made by the cooking fires. Some remained still because they were taking up positions and others darted in and out because they were helping with preparations. Finally, somewhere in the darkness, a horn or trumpet blew, and, simultaneously, a ring of torches on high poles was lit. Lud himself then appeared. He had changed into fresh clothes, although he still wore linen and not silk, and a light cloak was draped over his left arm. He surveyed his men and boys briefly and moved on to the pile of fleeces which had been arranged for him to lounge on.

'Where is my cup-bearer?' he called at once, despite the fact that his drinking horn and a flagon of wine were within two feet of him and he could very easily have helped himself.

'That's me, I think,' said Caleb to the cook who was in charge of him.

'Why didn't you say?' said the cook, alarmed. 'You're all grease. You stink.'

'Cup-bearer!'

'I'd better go.'

Lud eyed him thoughtfully. It was impossible not to notice the shiny grease spots.

'I've been making sure your meat is cooked exactly how you like it, O Great King. I had to lean right over the fire. That's why I'm...'

'You know how I like my meat, do you? Don't you also know that I like my servants clean?'

'I was really worried in case it got burnt.'

Lud said nothing more and, in the silence which followed, Caleb realised he was expected to do something. The wine! He filled the golden horn, bowed and handed it to the king who tilted it so fully that wine ran down each side of his great moustache.

'Are you feeling hungry now?'

There was no reply.

'I think the meat must be about done.'

Lud looked down into his drinking horn. More wine! Caleb poured it.

'It is true I am hungry,' said Lud and his cup-bearer was glad to leave him for the time being.

'He's hungry,' Caleb told the cook.

'You dare to call the Great King *he*?' The cook couldn't believe his ears. 'Take these,' and he gave Caleb a tray containing a plate of choice cuts of beef, the juicy bloody centre of the joint, a dish of vegetables and some hunks of bread.

Lud immediately threw the dish of vegetables over his shoulder.

'Animal fare,' he said and tossed a piece of beef at Caleb.

Caleb wasn't sure if this was more food the king couldn't abide or if it was a sign of Lud's favour. Was he being given a titbit like a favourite dog? The piece of meat had struck him on the neck and it rested half in the opening of his tunic. The hot pan juices were uncomfortable next to his skin. Slowly he retrieved the meat and put it in his mouth. Lud threw another piece which hit him in the eye and laughed. Caleb made himself laugh too.

Under the torchlight, the general feasting began. When Lud started to shout comments to his retainers about their performances during the day, this encouraged private conversations and jokes and soon there was a considerable din.

As he had promised, Lud gave away many presents to those who had fought well or thrown the best. He surprised Caleb by even having words for him: 'And you, my young ox, have my meat and my favour.' Then there was music. A blind harper came and sat beside the king who drooped into melancholy even before a single note had been played.

'Quench the torches!' he shouted. 'I want to hear the old songs and to think the old thoughts in darkness.'

Conversations died as the harper began. He sang of heroes and heroines who had lived, loved and fought all over the island of Britain. At the mention of two dragons who were eventually imprisoned amongst the stars, Lud suddenly called out, 'These stars of ours never change!' The harper plucked a few more notes and then stopped.

'In that world above us,' said the king, 'why should *their* stars make changing patterns? If the Summer lingers, their stars will never change again. Who remembers Cernunnos now?'

'Who is he?' 'I don't remember him,' said voices that were anxious to please.

'Flatterers, you remember him well,' mocked the king. 'Cernunnos who ran with the antlered creatures in Autumn. The god with horns whose season will not come again. He who called himself...'

'Jack Frost,' whispered Caleb.

'Who speaks the forbidden name?' asked Lud in a voice soft with menace.

Caleb swallowed.

'Do you miss him boy?'

'Perhaps a little,' said Caleb thinking it was what he was expected to say, but tensing for a blow all the same.

'Let us drink a farewell to Cernunnos, or *Jack*. None here can ever take in their hand that apple his long fingers would like to pinch.'

The fires burned low as the songs continued.

'I'll listen to just another, just one more, and then I'll slip away,' Caleb told himself, fascinated as he was by all the stories.

It wasn't safe for him to think of going until the flames had dwindled to almost nothing and Lud was beginning to nod.

The darkness might cover Caleb's escape, but it would also make it difficult for him to find his way back into the palace. He might bump into someone or fall down a flight of steps into a cellar, and yet he couldn't stay there.

CHAPTER FIFTEEN

Consequences

'I had a terrible time getting away,' said both children at once when they met again.

Blossom had been sitting by a window of the dusty upper room for hours it appeared before she heard the sound of footsteps she hoped were Caleb's. All kinds of thoughts had gone through her mind, the two most important being, 'Has he come back already and left without me?' and, 'Is he alive?'

There were only a few of the light-giving stones set in the ceiling of the room, but they were enough to show the entrance to Jack's passage. The children entered it with sighs of relief, hardly believing they were on the way home.

'That was Jack's doorstep we just passed over,' said Blossom after a while. 'Don't you feel better?' And soon they were staring at Jack himself who lay on the floor as if he hadn't moved for years.

'Are you all right?' asked Blossom pointlessly because he obviously wasn't.

'The apple is my cure-all,' he said in a dry rustle of a voice. 'Have you found it?'

'Not yet. But we've met the king and queen and we've survived to tell the tale,' said Caleb who couldn't help an edge of pride in his voice.

'For the first day that is perhaps enough. By the second and third days you must have their secrets.'

'No problem,' said Blossom, who wanted to cheer him up. 'You have something to eat and we'll see ourselves out.'

'I shall try to make the stairway to your world easier. Only hurry, I am very tired,' said Jack.

He did his best and, as the children climbed the steps to the Heath, they felt a force behind them pushing them on and lightening their efforts.

Caleb took his watch out of his pocket as they breathed in the night-time smells of Hampstead Heath.

'It's quarter to two!' he said. 'Mum and dad have probably got the police and the fire brigade and all the neighbours out looking for us.

'What are we going to tell them about your hair?' asked Blossom. 'They won't believe it was an accident. They'll nag and nag to find the name of the hairdresser so they can tell him off.'

'We've got to think of a reason for dyeing it,' said Caleb.

'We could say we were playing at being pop singers and they *always* have bleached hair.'

'Yes, and we thought it was the kind that washes out, but it isn't and we daren't go home. And then you've got to burst into tears because that always makes dad sympathetic.'

Blossom rehearsed a little and immediately found that real tears were coming in a flood.

'Every moment was so dangerous,' she said.

A uniformed policeman was talking very seriously to Mr Belling-Peake in the sitting room when they arrived home.

'I bleached my hair and we were afraid to come home,' shouted Caleb before any questions could be asked. He knew if the policeman said something as simple as, 'Well, young man?' he was sure to come out with the whole truth.

Blossom caused a useful distraction by having a sort of fit and going limp and Mrs Belling-Peake joined her in this as well as knocking over the tray of tea she had made for the police officer.

'I do apologise for all the trouble they've caused,' said Mr Belling-Peake wiping an eye with the back of his hand. The policeman said that he perfectly understood but he would just radio in to let a hell of a lot of people know they'd been wasting their time.

'I expect those kids of yours could hear us calling them all the time, but they didn't take a blind bit of notice,' he added.

Although Mrs Belling-Peake wanted to bathe, scold, feed and cuddle the children all at the same time, her husband persuaded her to take the actions in order. He scrubbed Caleb in one bathroom while Blossom was half suffocated with shampoo in the other.

'All pop stars have to have blond hair,' explained Caleb. 'When it didn't wash out, we hid in a bush and it got later and later.'

'I've rubbed half your scalp off and it hasn't made a bit of difference,' said his father.

Then there was hot chocolate in the kitchen and Blossom regurgitated hers which she was always likely to do when under stress.

'I think we ought to draw a firm line under today and forget it,' said Mr Belling-Peake. 'What with the cellar and all.'

'What's wrong with the cellar, dad?' asked Caleb, alert to a change of subject.

'Oh, I had to go down there for some boxes this morning and it's damp and mildewy and smelly. I've always maintained we're over a watercourse.'

'A river!'

'Not exactly. You know the Fleet River runs under a lot of Hampstead and that its two main tributaries flow beneath the Heath itself?'

Of course Caleb knew. Who better, because he had stepped over one of those very tributaries that afternoon.

'There must be scores of unmapped little streams that feed the Fleet and we live above one. That's my theory, at any rate,' continued his father. 'Though why there should be excess water when it's so hot, I can't begin to guess. Nothing about the climate or the weather makes sense at the moment.'

It did make sense, however, and Caleb and Blossom knew what that sense was. They also knew what the result would be if they told their parents a hundredth part of it.

CHAPTER SIXTEEN

Gathering Strength

Not unexpectedly, the children slept late the next morning. The relief of being in their own beds cancelled out any feelings of urgency concerning Jack.

'Dad and I have been thinking,' said Mrs Belling-Peake when Caleb appeared in the kitchen, 'What upset us most about last night was that you didn't dare come home. Stiff white hair seems to be the thing nowadays, so why should we make a fuss?'

Caleb felt ill with guilt. How could his parents think *they* were in the wrong? If he'd had a son who stayed out all night, he would have kicked him up and down the stairs.

'We've got a den on the Heath. We were perfectly safe. And we're really sorry.'

'No, *we're* sorry, darling,' said his mother. 'Would you like breakfast in the garden? It's almost as hot as July out there.'

'I'll fetch Blossom so we can have it together.'

'I've decided today is a rest day,' he told his sister when he woke her up.

'Good idea,' said Blossom. 'I couldn't face Kigva today.'

'Hallowe'en is on Wednesday, though,' said Caleb. 'We can't have any more days off.'

They sat at the garden table *comparing notes*, which is how Blossom described her cheating at school. Very little came of this, so they played with the cat who was always affectionate when there was food on the table. They came to the conclusion that, although they had got to know the personalities of Lud and Brigantia, they had gained no real clues as to the whereabouts of the silver hand and the apple.

'Dad,' said Blossom when Mr Belling-Peake came into the garden to air some things he had taken out of the cellar, 'Who is Epona?'

'Epona? A horse goddess of the Ancient Britons. Why?'

'She was mentioned in a lesson at school.

'Legends said that her father was a god and her mother a mare. The Ancient Britons, or Celts, were always drawing cartoon figures of horses on cups and hillsides. I expect they burnt people in honour of her.'

Blossom became very thoughtful.

'Talking of burning,' continued her father, 'I could happily set fire to that Mr Frost who came to dinner. You remember him. We talked of bringing out a really interesting book together and now he's disappeared from the face of the earth, taking my good ideas with him.'

'Have you heard of Cernunnos?' asked Caleb quickly.

'Another Celtic god. One who's depicted with a stag's antlers on his head.'

'You mean he's a monster?'

'All ancient gods were monsters, weren't they?' said his father brightly and went indoors.

'What shall we do now?' Blossom asked the cat. 'What if I meet Epona.'

Caleb didn't tell her that Cernunnos was their Jack Frost in another guise.

'You won't meet her,' he said unconvincingly. 'She'd be too embarrassed to be seen if she was half a horse. Anyway, you said Kigva looked normal.'

'I'm not sure now. I only saw her with her clothes on.'

Their mother called from the kitchen window, 'Has one of you been throwing things away down the waste disposal?'

'No,' said Caleb.

'That's what Brigantia said,' remarked Blossom.

'What?'

'That she'd thrown the silver hand away.'

'You didn't tell me that.'

'It's not important. We *know* she threw it away.'

'We don't know it at all. Jack said he thought she'd hidden it. Don't you see?'

'No.'

'When you say you've thrown something away, you mean you've thrown it down, like into a hole.'

'We must ask Jack if he knows of any holes. Tomorrow.'

'Yes, tomorrow,' said Caleb.

'Let's go over what the king said to you again,' suggested Blossom.

'He couldn't make up his mind if he wanted people to talk about Jack or not. He almost told me to say I missed him.'

Their father came outside.

'I don't want you children going into the cellar until further notice,' he said. 'It isn't at all healthy down there.'

'So that's what Lud meant,' said Caleb when Mr Belling-Peake had disappeared again.

'Tell me.'

'He seemed kind of sorry he stole the apple, but you'd think from the way he said it there was nothing he could do about it. He said nobody from down there could get the apple back. That must mean it's somewhere unhealthy for them. I thought he was just saying it was well hidden.'

'That's not all, Caleb. Nobody from there can get it back. But we're not from there. I mean, *you're* not, so you could get it back, couldn't you?'

'Not today though.'

'Jack's lucky to have us and he's too tired to make those horrid spots on our hands hurt when we're not in the mood,' said Blossom confidently.

As they took their breakfast things into the kitchen, the telephone rang again. Friends of the family were saying how pleased they were that the children had come to no harm. Mrs Belling-Peake was anxious to change the subject. 'We're having trouble with our cellar too,' she said into the receiver. 'Rupert says he thinks it's an underground stream.'

The conversation at lunchtime and throughout the afternoon between Mr and Mrs Belling-Peake and over the telephone with their friends was of underground water and smells. As their parents were always very worried by problems concerning the house, the children were able to keep to themselves and avoid hearing the phrase that, above all others, they dreaded:

'You are not to go onto the Heath again.'

CHAPTER SEVENTEEN

A Door Closes

By Monday morning they felt strong - as strong as you are ever likely to feel at the prospect of going into a country where they have magical powers and you don't, where you are frightened silly of being found out and where, by the way, you have to put the seasons to rights.

The star in the grass had almost entirely gone - it was so indistinct they couldn't really tell whether they were in the right place at all. There was clearly no going down that way. Remembering the last time, they threw themselves at every patch of early morning shade, but it was no use - the shade remained shade and their ankles soon hurt from their having jumped up and down so hard.

'It's no good,' said Caleb. 'Jack's given us up as a bad job. He must've got tired of waiting.'

'That's that then. Perhaps he's found the apple and the silver hand himself,' said Blossom, relieved but offended.

Then her face took on the expression it had when Caleb told her she had just eaten a maggot in her peach. A *thing* was coming out of the bushes behind her brother and she couldn't get the words out to warn him in time. He thought she was getting ready for a gigantic sneeze until an animal hand boxed him on the ear from behind. When he turned, yellow eyes were no more than a yard from his. The *thing* had antlers and it was pawing the ground with cloven feet as if preparing to run at them. There was no escaping, but they threw themselves away from the animal all the same. Within seconds, it had driven them into a tree trunk. This was one of Jack Frost's tree trunks, however, and they passed directly through the bark and were soon spinning down into Jack's world.

'You are nothing but children indeed,' said Jack, who had resumed the shape they generally knew him by.

'There was no need to frighten us,' said Caleb. 'We needed a day off.'

'Next time you look like that, I shall set some dogs on you,' said Blossom whose anger had made her brave.

'We have all been angry. Let us be friends now,' said Jack. 'I thought to punish you with fear.'

'Well, you shouldn't have made Blossom throw up. She'll be funny all day.'

Jack crumpled beside his table. 'I feel that this has taken the rest of my strength,' he said.

'While we're on the subject of you,' said Blossom, 'Dad is very disappointed.'

'That is of no importance to me,' said Jack. 'Now change out of those outlandish clothes.'

'Jack, you've deliberately left my clothes all mucky. I smell of old cooking,' said Caleb as he started to dress.

'I am not your laundress.'

'We've come to some conclusions,' said Blossom when she reappeared from changing.

'Yes, we're pretty sure the silver hand has been thrown down somewhere and the apple is in a dangerous place where your people can't go.'

'But Caleb could go there,' added Blossom.

'You keep on saying that.'

'You have learnt nothing,' said Jack. 'These conclusions I could have told you from the start. You must try again.'

'How measly!' said Blossom. 'If you knew Brigantia had dropped the hand down a hole, why didn't you go around looking in all the holes you could find? There can't be that many. It's not a very big kingdom, after all.'

'Come on,' said Caleb. 'We've got work to do.'

అ ఆ

Caleb made his way down to the front entrance of King Lud's half of the palace expecting to see the usual morning panic to get out onto the grass first. Nothing of the sort was happening. Men and boys stood in thoughtful huddles looking nervously at the door which led outside and at the one which led further inside the palace, as if something appalling was likely to burst through them.

Little notice was taken of Caleb as he slipped from one huddle to another, listening and picking up nothing useful. The men in charge occasionally went outside and their faces were eagerly searched when they returned as if they might have the good news that everyone wanted. They had glum faces each time they came back and sometimes they even ran in waving their hands rapidly around their heads. Caleb realised something very peculiar was up and that everyone else present knew what it was. After a good half hour of being the only person not in on the secret, he sidled around a group of boys and peeped out of the doorway. Nothing seemed any different from before.

'Ow!' he said as a mosquito sucked deeply on the fleshy tip of his ear.

'Been bitten by one of your own kind, have you?' said Arawn who had been standing in the doorway with folded arms and looking seriously at a point far away.

'You cause as much trouble as a stinging fly.'

He casually pulled Caleb towards him by the sleeve, holding him only by two calloused fingers to make the point that he was almost too filthy to touch.

'We need a messenger to take our news to the king.'

'What exactly should I say, sir?'

What *could* he say when he had no idea what was wrong?

'You're so clever, you can think of the words. They're bound to amuse the king.'

'I wouldn't want to let you down, sir.'

'It's *sir*, is it, when Lud's not here to take your side? Tell him that the ground is more marshy than yesterday. The water has risen higher and this morning there are flies. Ask him where he wants to take his breakfast. It's impossible outside.'

He smacked Caleb on the neck and held the remains of wings and a sultana-sized body up for his inspection.

'They seem to like you. I'm not surprised. Now go and deliver your message, little fly.'

He flicked Caleb back inside the palace. The groups of boys and men parted, clearing a line towards the large door in the centre of one wall so that it was obvious where Caleb had to go to speak to the king.

He tried to look proud of his errand, but, never in his life, had so many people stared at him in such an unfriendly manner. He could feel the jealous malice of the boys and the scorn of the men beating on him. His plan was to shut the door firmly behind him, slam it if he dared, and then, if the way to Lud's private apartments wasn't clear, to sneak off and hide. Fortunately, on the other side of the door was a staircase which had to lead somewhere important. At the top was a corridor and, trusting his instinct, as Jack had told them to do, he set off along it. King Lud appeared simultaneously in the doorway at the end of the corridor and Caleb ran towards him, confident of a warm reception.

'I have a message from Lord Arawn, Great King,' he said, stressing Arawn's name so that Lud would know exactly who to blame if the message put him in a bad humour. Lud swept by him, apparently deaf, and Caleb, having stood for a few moments in a state of shock, had to chase after him.

'Arawn says there's more water, and flies too, so you can't go outside.'

'The Lord Arawn would not use the word *can't* to his king.'

'Sorry. I mean sorry, Great King.'

'You were not here yesterday to fill my cup. Are boys so lazy now that they must sleep all day and not do their work?'

'I'll work very hard today. I promise.'

'You will never come in my sight again. I do not give my favour to have it valued at no more than these flies you mention. Go back to sleep wrapped in the refuse of the kitchen. I have disturbed one Sleeper, why should I disturb another?'

Here was disaster. As the door crashed shut behind the king, Caleb sank down onto the stairs. It was all Jack's fault. If he had given him a clean set of clothes to wear, Lud wouldn't have pushed him aside. Kings understandably didn't want ragamuffins near them and how was he going to hear Lud's secrets when he wasn't even allowed in the same room?

One of the older boys came out of the room Lud had entered.

'The king says you must be chained up and work in the kitchen. It's what you deserve. I'm to tell the cook.'

Laughing, he walked towards Caleb whose first instinct was to mutter, 'Help me Jack! Help me Jack!' as the time when all hope was lost seemed to have arrived. No help came. No shield of magic protected him and the boy easily twisted Caleb's thinner, weaker arms behind his back.

'I hope that water keeps rising and rising and the flies are deadly poisonous.'

The boy laughed again and pushed Caleb's elbows up behind him in a more painful hold. They went into the kitchen as the cook was turning away from the fire with a pan of spitting fat.

'It's him, is it?' said the cook. 'Got a bit above himself, did he?'

'The king says chain him tightly to the spit so he can work it all day long.'

'He didn't say *tightly*,' said Caleb.

'He said *very tightly*, so there are red rings on his arms.'

The cook stood there enjoying Caleb's misery, the fat swilling from side to side in the pan.

'I'll have him done to a turn, like the meat.'

'You won't!'

Although it meant lowering his back and causing a sharp pain to race through his twisted shoulders, Caleb managed to swing a foot up under the pan of fat. It sprayed over the cook's apron front and his bare arms. As the boy and the cook's other assistants went to the aid of the yelling man, Caleb made his escape. Here was the end of his adventure. He was a hunted boy, one surely with a price on his head and one likely to be punished with the greatest severity if he was caught.

CHAPTER EIGHTEEN

Brigantia

No message had been sent to Queen Brigantia. How could they knock on her door and say, 'Excuse me, madam, but your picnic ground has turned into a swamp'?

They spread her silken carpets on the driest patch of grass they could find and hoped for the best, only the best didn't happen.

The queen was halfway towards her throne of cushions before she sensed a stickiness and dampness underfoot. She stopped and shook one of her feet, as if this would make things better. While her foot was off the ground, the hollow left behind in the carpet filled with half an inch of water. When the royal foot was put down again, there was a splash. The hem of her dress had dragged in water too and brushed heavily against her legs. Together, she and her attendants stood stiff with shock as, beneath them, the ruined carpets subsided into the sloppiness. Brigantia struggled to decide whether to be bewildered or angry.

'Are we on a quicksand?' she asked. 'Someone explain.'

Kigva darted forward and splashed onto her knees, the water striking the queen's dress quite high up.

'We thought it was a dry spot, O Great Queen. It's wet everywhere. The water just keeps coming up through the ground.'

'At the height of Summer? It isn't logical. No, it's magic, Lud's doing. It's called *getting even*.' She straightened her back.

'Girls, act as if nothing has happened, as if the ground is dry as a bone. He is *not* going to see me look uncomfortable.'

She turned and faced Lud's doorway where there was almost no activity. Then, she said in a penetrating voice, 'Let's be generous this morning. We *always* beat the king, so why not let *him* play outside for once. Inside, girls, and,' dropping her voice to an urgent whisper, 'if I catch anyone looking as if we've been made to go, you know the nasty sorts of thing I can dream up.'

She splashed off, her head high, and expected her girls to do the same. One lost her footing, slipped and fell full length, crying out immediately afterwards, 'Ugh, I'm all wet.'

Brigantia turned round slowly. 'Are you wet, my child? That is strange, the ground being so dry. Of course, you must have spilt something over yourself, a jug of milk perhaps.'

A quantity of milk appeared over the tactless girl's head and swept down her, making her hair and her thin dress cling tightly.

'A bit sour, isn't it? Lumpy too. What's that you said? It was a jug of apple juice you spilt and a bucket of pond water *and* a full tub of dripping that was just about to set. What a butterfingers.'

As each suggestion was made, a cloud of liquid appeared above the girl like a shapeless hat and then drenched her. She had learned her lesson and knew better than to cry out or sob, although she could hardly have been more uncomfortable.

'You'll have to be more careful in future and not have such shaky fingers. Look what a state you're in.

'Forgive me, O Great Queen.'

'We'll sort through my wardrobe today. I've been meaning to do it for a long time. And he needn't think I'm going to let him get away with this. Oh never. No!' So saying, she led her train indoors.

The queen made a small and snappish breakfast and

Blossom was able to keep well away from her, warned by the example of the poor girl coated in hardening dripping who wasn't allowed to change her clothes. If there was to be another candidate for a cascade of sour milk or pond water or worse, she imagined it was bound to be herself and she was glad to be sent on errands to the kitchen as the queen rejected most of the dainty dishes set before her.

Afterwards, the court moved upstairs to the queen's bedroom and dressing rooms. Brigantia and her most important attendants went into the bedroom and the lesser girls were detailed to fetch clothing as it was required. As soon as it was clear that there were to be two teams - one outside and one inside the bedroom - Blossom volunteered to be on the inside. She knew she couldn't stay away from the queen's bad temper all day if she was to discover what had happened to the silver hand.

'You must learn,' said Enid. 'The girls are all in order and you're right at the bottom. You can't attend the queen. Help me instead.'

'I want to be near the queen. I'm very quick at undoing clothes.'

She meant, 'I *have* to be near the queen, to save Jack, to save all of us.'

'It's dangerous.' said Enid.

'I don't mind a little bit of dripping.'

'One girl was never seen again, but a sad little dog appeared in the palace one day. Come with me before the others take too much notice of you. Kigva has a long memory.'

Struggling, despite the story of the little dog, Blossom was pulled into one of the dressing rooms, a plain chamber full of chests and wardrobes.

Kigva stood importantly at the bedroom door relaying the queen's orders and shouting at the others.

'Bring all the cloaks.' 'The queen wants to try on

everything blue.' 'The contents of the largest chest and get a move on.'

For a while, as Brigantia was dressed and undressed and draped with precious stones and told how beautiful she looked, there was even a light-hearted mood. Blossom and Enid helped unlock the wardrobes and lift the lids of chests, humming as they went about their work. Enid kept repeating snatches of a tune that Blossom found easy to hum along with. They carried each garment between them so that it didn't catch and tear or drag along the floor. Blossom could have caressed the clothes for hours if she had been left alone, but she had to be content with the brief feel as they carried them for the haughty Kigva's approval.

And then the queen became bored and irritable. Her hour of calm conversation with her girls had been no more than the lull before a typhoon. She started to complain that they were slow, that they didn't mean it when they said she looked wonderful in a particular necklace, that their fingers were cold.

'No wonder your mother won't let you attend her,' she shouted at Kigva. 'When I asked for the clothes with lilies on, I didn't mean the Winter clothes as well. I shall never need Winter clothes again, so why show me furs and these heavy shoes?'

'It was the fault of those stupid girls who are bringing the clothes, O Great Queen. They made the mistake.'

'If you gave them proper instructions, it wouldn't matter that they're stupid. Stop trying to shift the blame. Now you're getting in my way!'

She pushed Kigva aside and strode to the first of the dressing rooms where Enid and Blossom were at work.

'It had to be you,' said the queen contemptuously to Blossom. 'These are Winter clothes and I never want to see them again.'

She seized hold of a pile of dresses Enid had neatly folded on a chest top and threw them up into the air. On their downward journey, they draped themselves over the two nervous girls.

'Don't move,' said Enid.

'No, don't move,' said the queen. 'And when you whisper about me, make sure I can't hear.'

As Enid and Blossom stood temporarily blinded by the dresses wrapped around their heads, they could hear the creaking of wardrobe doors being hurled back and chest lids being thrown open and the swish as countless articles of clothing were tossed to the ceiling. Eventually there was the crash as the door of the room was slammed and the raised voice of the queen retreated down the passage outside.

'Quickly,' said Enid. 'When she has one of these tempers, she expects everything to be tidied up at once. We'll take the Winter clothes to another room and the Summer ones have to be refolded.'

When their work was done, Enid said, 'They say the queen doesn't want to be disturbed. That's a bad sign. It was all that water outside. She hates looking foolish.'

These were the worst words Blossom could have heard - *Do not disturb*. They were worse even than *I'm going to coat you in dripping*. There had to be a way of eavesdropping on the queen and she was determined to find it. Although she trusted Enid and was sure the girl knew perfectly well that she came from the world above, she was afraid to drop any hints of her quest. Enid might have sworn to report to the queen anyone asking about the silver hand.

'I don't expect she's that cross really,' said Blossom. 'Couldn't we take her some cakes and a cup of - drink? She'll say *That's just what I wanted* and be nice to us.'

She had been about to say *cup of tea*!

'No-one is safe who crosses her path for the rest of the day,' said Enid. 'Kigva is only safe because her mother is Epona.'

Blossom pulled a face. 'I might as well go - and be by myself then.'

She had almost said *I might as well go home*. If she was jittery and likely to let the truth about herself slip, perhaps she *was* safer away.

'You must do what you think is best,' said Enid, clearly meaning, *And don't tell me about it.*

'I'll go for a little walk,' said Blossom.

'Yes,' and Enid turned her back so she had no idea of the direction Blossom took.

Blossom carefully made her way up the main staircase of Brigantia's half of the palace, looking behind her as she went. When she reached the floors of empty rooms, she smiled and began to hum to herself again. It was good to be going home during the hours of daylight, even though she had achieved nothing and learnt nothing. Coming down into the kingdom of Lud and Brigantia was like going to the dentist's. The more you did it, the easier it *didn't* become. Why was it so wrong to have fine, sunny days all year round, she asked herself. What was so good about penetrating cold and frozen noses? How lovely to laze on a beach at any time of year and be able to wade out amongst flapping rags of seaweed, looking for anemones and glistening, patterned stones whenever the fancy took you. Then there was this other kind of water - this unwelcome kind filtering up from who knew where. It was in their cellar at home and in Lud's fields, as if every surface of the Earth, too hot by far, was giving out an unhealthy sweat. This water, she was sure, was some kind of warning, despite Brigantia's assertion that it was only Lud playing magical tricks.

She hummed on as she was thinking all this and then suddenly stopped with a gasp and scratched at the banister. That tune she and Enid had shared, she knew it. 'Enid,' she said in a tone of regret or sympathy and made a half-turn downwards again. No, it was too much to cope with, and Enid was bound to be there tomorrow for her to suggest the plan that had flashed through her mind. Running away from her thoughts, she went as fast as she could up the remaining stairs and, to her surprise, found Caleb sitting dirty and miserable at the top.

He burst into tears as she appeared and, given such an example, Blossom could only copy him. Half of what they said to each other was obscured by chokes and snuffles.

'I think I've killed someone,' said Caleb.

'What!'

'I threw boiling hot fat at him. He wanted to chain me up in the kitchen.'

'That'll teach him. Anyway, they can use magic to make him better.'

'I hadn't thought of that.'

'But poor Enid.'

'Who?'

'You know, my friend. She kept singing a song and I joined in because I knew it but I didn't know I knew it till just now when I remembered and it's *Sweet Phyllis Goes A-maying* that we're learning at school so it means she could have been down here since Elizabethan times because it was written then and I think she's human and I should have gone back for her but I couldn't be bothered.'

The rush of information left Caleb confused.

'They're keeping her a prisoner,' said Blossom. 'Why didn't I go back when I thought of it! We could take her home.'

'Perhaps she's happy down here.'

'Happy! They're all so spiteful. The queen's always shouting and now she refuses to see anyone so I haven't got an earthly chance of finding out where she's hidden the silver hand.'

'It's worse for me. Lud says he doesn't want me near him any more - OR ELSE, because I'm dirty and always asleep.'

'Oh Caleb, let's go and ask Jack what to do.'

Jack was sipping a cup of drink when they arrived. He lay on the floor and looked up in surprise.

'Jack, it's all gone wrong,' said Blossom slumping onto the fleeces beside him. 'May I have some of your drink?'

'You won't like this, but Lud has told me to keep away from him,' said Caleb. 'So what's the point in going back?'

'I am trying to restore myself,' said Jack. 'You are learning nothing and I may have to go amongst them myself, though it will surely mean the end of me.'

'Don't say that. We'll try harder. It's just that we haven't got very far today.'

'Jack, are there any people, I mean real people like Caleb and me, living down here?'

'There are some. Every century one or two tumble through our gates. They should know better.'

'Can they get out again?'

'All you need to know is that *you* can return to your home now because you have been chosen. Be gone and do better tomorrow.'

He could offer them little help with their upward journey and it was two weary children who reappeared in a bramble thicket on the Heath some time afterwards.

CHAPTER NINETEEN

Escape in Prospect

Mr Belling-Peake stared at the main headline in the *Evening Standard* which said: '**HAMPSTEAD'S BIG STINK**'.

'How would you two like a surprise holiday?' he asked his children, expecting whoops of delight rather than the looks of suspicion he actually received.

'What do you mean?' said Caleb.

'Hampstead is becoming too unhealthy by half. Look at the paper. Stand in the street and sniff. Mum and I think we ought to get away.'

'Get away!'

'Until the Council flushes out its drains and gets rid of the typhoid and whatever, it would be a good idea if we popped down to Cornwall.'

'Cornwall!'

'We've telephoned Owen and Carol and they say there's no-one in the cottage. You didn't think you would be spending October on a beach, did you? Or visiting the castle, Caleb.'

As Blossom had only recently been thinking of sand and fun, she wondered whether someone with special powers had been listening to her thoughts. She loved the cottage they often stayed in.

'I need some peace and quiet to finish my book,' said Mrs Belling-Peake and immediately brought Blossom to her senses. The worst torment in the world was to be locked up with Poppy Shandy when she was in the middle of a story about ladybirds or robins who had forgotten how to fly. It was, 'Darling, just listen to this,' and 'I know you're in suspense about the next part of the story,' when all you really wanted was for the ladybird to be run over on the next page.

'We don't want to go to Cornwall,' said Blossom, knowing she was speaking for her brother too.

'We're all right here,' added Caleb.

'What an abrupt and ungrateful pair. Offer them a holiday and they snap at you. If I decide we're going, then the negative attitude of two spoilt children doesn't enter into it.'

Mr Belling-Peake crumpled the newspaper and threw it unsuccessfully at the waste paper bin.

'You and mum go if you like. We can stay with Auntie Marion.'

'Since when has she been *Auntie*? You always shy away from poor Marion when she's trying to be affectionate.'

'Oh mum, we're having such a good time on the Heath,' said Blossom. 'We've found ever so many new places to hide and explore.'

'You're out there till all hours, going without lunch. You're not secretly drinking or smoking are you?' asked Mrs Belling-Peake thinking that a short break in Cornwall might be the best idea for everyone.

'Mum!'

Blossom was beside herself with indignation. She became hot, red and breathless all at once and didn't know whether to shout at her parents that she hated them for being so suspicious, or to smash the pot of jam that stood within easy reach on the edge of the table. It was a year since she and Caleb had stolen a bottle of wine and a packet of Marion's cigarettes and made themselves sick.

'Calm down, Blossom. Mum didn't mean it.'

Blossom found it very hard to be calm.

'I'd rather die than go to Cornwall and listen to those stories about ladybirds,' she said, almost out of control and knowing her mother would be very hurt. 'If you make arrangements behind our backs, I shall run away for ever.'

Then she ran up to her bedroom and jumped up and down on the floor for a quite a long time.

'What have you two been getting up to, Caleb?' asked Mr Belling-Peake after his wife had gone upstairs to look after Blossom and the ceiling. He realised that no normal circumstances could make his daughter react in this mad way.

Caleb would have loved to tell his father the whole story. Together, they could have gone down and banged some sense into the heads of the king and queen. When he and Blossom were in the palace, they lived in fear of being turned into a puff of smoke, and at home they had to tell lies all the time. It was an uncomfortable situation. But there was no chance of their parents believing them, although Mr Belling-Peake published books about ancient mythology. Despite all the fairy stories written by Poppy Shandy, Mrs Belling-Peake would have telephoned for a doctor or the police if Caleb said they had met a man calling himself Jack Frost.

Caleb put together his story very carefully.

'We're playing at gods and goddesses and magic. That's why we asked you about those old names.'

'Oh yes. You can play that sort of game anywhere. Cornwall is a much more magical place than London. It's a Celtic country, after all, and you were asking me about the Celtic gods.'

'We've got our own magic trees and areas and things on the Heath.'

'You can have whole ranges of hills and woods in Cornwall for your magic.'

'They're useless.'

'Don't be contradictory. In fact, go to your room. You and your sister have been running too wild of late. Look at your hair. It's about time we kept a closer eye on you.'

Keeping a closer eye meant a telephone call to Cornwall during the evening and a corner of a sleeping tablet being crushed secretly into Blossom's hot chocolate. Caleb managed to sneak out of his bedroom and listen to the telephone conversation. So, plans for the escape from London were going ahead.

Mr Belling-Peake said to Owen, 'This underground water is undoubtedly germ-laden. I'm getting the family away tomorrow morning. People who lived by the Fleet River in the last century regularly went down with tuberculosis and typhoid, you know. By the way, don't expect two particularly cheerful children. For reasons best known to themselves, they want to stay at home.'

After thinking so hard his eyes ached, Caleb decided he had two major choices. He could run away by night with Blossom in tow (He was unaware she had been mildly drugged.), or he could enlist whatever remained of Jack Frost's powers. If he managed to contact Jack at all and ask him to stop the planned excursion, he was afraid Jack's remedy might be too drastic. The cottage in Cornwall could catch fire, or a tree in the street outside could fall on their car, with or without his parents in it. It was an enormous risk when he knew how much store Jack set by having Brigantia's apple before Samhain. If, on the other hand, he went down to Lud's kingdom now, on Monday night, he would have to stay there until they had succeeded or failed because, if he returned home in the meantime, his father wouldn't let him out of his sight again.

But what was there for him to achieve below the Heath? He had fallen out of favour with the king and could hardly spend two days creeping along the corridors of the palace and hiding in cupboards hoping that people would have meaningful conversations right outside the door.

Blossom's last question to Jack also niggled in his brain: *Can human beings who find their way down here get out again?* If he was captured by Lud, and Jack had faded away, who would help him? Was it right to expose his sister to this danger when she had made an enemy too?

'Are you still sulking in there, Caleb?'

'I'm not sulking.'

'That's good. What peculiar children I have. You must take after me.'

Mrs Belling-Peake sat on the edge of Caleb's bed swinging three odd socks she had found. 'I've nearly finished the packing,' she said. 'You've chosen a very bad evening to annoy dad. Don't get on his nerves tomorrow or we'll have the most unimaginable drive to Cornwall.'

'Was he upset already?' in the little boy voice of insincere sympathy.

'Julian has been teasing him about the book he isn't going to write with the disappearing Mr Frost. Dad was rather short with him.'

'Are we leaving early?'

'About eight if we can.'

'I'll get ready for bed then.'

'There's a good boy.'

When his mother, trustingly, had gone, Caleb took some coins from the pot of change on his chest of drawers and crept downstairs. A third and better plan had come to him at last.

'Going somewhere?'

His father caught him before he reached the door.

'I'm looking for Percy. I want him to sleep on the end of my bed. Is Marion going to feed him while we're away?'

There was a stay of execution as the telephone rang.

'Don't move an inch while I answer that.'

Caleb sat on the floor and played unhappily with his ten pence pieces. His plan had been shot down in flames.

'Well,' said Mr Belling-Peake with satisfaction when he had put down the receiver. 'I'm delaying the holiday for twenty-four hours. That was Mr Frost. He's had some problems at home so he couldn't keep in touch. Now he's free again and he's invited himself to lunch tomorrow to talk about our book.'

'That's good news.'

'It's good news for you at this very moment because I've decided not to shout at you for trying to slip out.'

Jack had forestalled him. This had been Caleb's plan, to go to the call-box on Rosslyn Hill and impersonate Mr Frost. Jack could hear when he wanted to. What a pity he had chosen not to hear when Caleb called for help that morning.

CHAPTER TWENTY

Triple Trouble

Blossom learnt of the postponement of the holiday as she was tucking into her second breakfast helping of bananas on toast.

'We won't get in the way when Jack's here,' said Caleb. 'Hurry up.'

On the Heath, the door to Lud's kingdom proved elusive yet again.

'I'm fed up with him,' said Blossom. 'If he could make that telephone call to say he was coming to lunch, when we know he won't, he could jolly well make those steps appear.'

'He did once say he had to be careful in case someone spotted him. I can't remember who it was.'

'It began with *Bel*. Jack said he was the sun god and of course he'd like the Summer to last for ever and ever.'

'Perhaps we shouldn't be talking about him out loud.'

'Caleb, this is *our* world, not Jack's. That's our sun. It's millions of miles away. Look at it. It's not a god.'

Blossom dropped a mock curtsey and stared up into the sky.

'Hello, Mr Bel. We're Jack Frost's friends. Would you like to know all about us? I'm Blossom and this...'

'Belenos!'

A rumbling voice filled the air around them and the indistinct edge of the sun's disc began to look like hair. Blossom felt she might have acted very rashly.

'Belenos!'

The orb of the sun was now clearly a head and a golden sky-body was forming below it. A whole drop of the sun hung in the air above them, condensing into limbs and outstretched hands.

'Belenos!'

'You've given it all away, Blossom. Jack! Jack! Cernunnos!'

Long flame fingers floated behind them and the bright band in front was a thumb.

'Ja...'

But the ground had swallowed them where they stood.

'Belenos has widened his eyes for days,' said Jack. 'You had no need to taunt him. Now all time and secrecy are lost.'

He pushed Caleb, in his new, clean clothes, out of the room.

'Though he must stay in the sky by day, by night he will make his way to Lud's fireside and reveal all my scheming. Think of my power now as the last bead of drink on a cup's rim. Belenos will shake me off when darkness falls. Be gone!'

They had less of a plan in their heads than on any of the other days. Caleb was, presumably, to try and keep a red-hot stranger away from the king and Blossom was to - what?

This was just what Blossom asked herself when she arrived downstairs and found nothing going on. The queen was locked in her room still and the girls sat about waiting for instructions. Something had happened to make Kigva more unbearably grand than ever and so Blossom went in search of Enid to be given up-to-date news. There was no Enid in the kitchen, nor in any of the chambers on the ground floor.

'You're not allowed up there today,' said Kigva as Blossom set out to look for her friend in the queen's dressing rooms.

'Why not?'

'Serving girls don't ask *Why not?*'

'I'm looking for Enid.'

'Poor Enid.'

'What's happened to her? You look pleased.'

'I'd be more pleased if it happened to you. My mother, the great goddess Epona, and the queen are working magic together and we all have to keep away. Actually, I could take part too because I'm a goddess's daughter, but they don't want to show favouritism.'

'Ha, ha!' said Blossom. 'They don't want you either.'

She knew she shouldn't be wasting her time in quarrels with Kigva and making life difficult for herself, but the girl was so awful she had to be answered back.

'I'll tell you what's happened to your friend Enid. It's the funniest story I've heard in a long time. She thought she'd dropped one of her nasty bracelets near the queen's bedroom yesterday and when she went back to look for it she was caught snooping. The queen said if she wanted so badly to know about the magic going on, she could have some of it all to herself. That's all we've heard, but we know she's been locked away and we think the queen's worked a really horrible spell on her. I can guess what it is.'

Kigva didn't obstruct Blossom's way to the queen's apartments and seemed almost to be challenging her to go where she wasn't meant to. Her eyes and her little smile said, *I dare you*, and Blossom's glare and her tight mouth said, equally strongly, *Yes I do dare and you know how much I'd like to smack your face really hard.*

She slowly walked up the little branch staircase that ended in the corridor to Brigantia's bedroom. If only she had come back for Enid yesterday, she could have spared her the punishment that Kigva found so amusing. She hardly dared think what it might be.

'Mother! Mother! There's a servant girl listening outside,' shouted Kigva as Blossom stood indecisively, not knowing whether to investigate the rooms leading off the corridor or to screw her courage into her fist and rat-a-tat on the queen's door. She turned round to pull a face at the source of the tale-telling, who had darted back out of sight, and found the staircase end of the corridor receding from her as she was blown or sucked towards the queen's bedroom. She didn't even feel herself pass through the door.

Inside, although it was very dark, she sensed that there were several other people present. She was held immobile with her arms firmly at her sides by some invisible power rather than by physical hands.

'Shall we let the guilty thing speak?' cawed a voice.

'Oh yes, let her speak. She might tell us lies and then we can play with her.'

As Blossom became more accustomed to the darkness, she made out the bent shape of Brigantia in her form of the crone, the warty, wrinkled form that had so frightened her. With the queen were two other similarly ancient creatures. If only she could have kicked or raced round the room several times, it would have allowed some release of the terror that seemed to fill her mind two or three times over. When she tried to close her eyes and escape inside herself, she found that even her eyeballs were under the influence of magic and she couldn't avoid looking at these hags who were enjoying their power to terrify her.

In the middle of the bedroom floor was a cauldron of water over which the three goddesses, Brigantia, Epona and one whose name Blossom didn't know, had been weaving a spell.

A puff of red mist came off the water and one of the goddesses said, 'The water clears. Leave her. The water clears.'

Brigantia flourished her hands over the surface of the water. She chanted her spell:

Poison from a tainted well
Identify the king's great spell.

'It is still too murky. Lud does not want us to know the magic he has used.'

'Come nearer while we are waiting, child. It may frighten you to death.'

Blossom was forced to approach the cauldron and bend her head over it.

'Something living to clear the water properly. If the chicken is not enough, we always have this new little bird my daughter sent along.'

There was a brief scuffling and squawking away from the cauldron and then a black, limp, headless object slopped into the water.

'That's doing the trick nicely. Look, Little Yellow Hair. We won't need your head after all.'

A spiral of red in the water coalesced into a circle which in turn became very clearly an apple. The vision lasted no more than a minute and Blossom was once again looking at a mass of bedraggled feathers and a chicken's yellow feet bobbing upside down.

'He has never made my anger rise higher than this,' said Brigantia.

'You must not let him have the last word. He is sending the water into the palace itself now. Find the spell and break the spell.'

Epona took Blossom's hand in her scaly, knotted claw.

'We still haven't heard from our visitor. We're relying on you to tell us how King Lud makes the water rise.'

At first, Blossom couldn't find the words. Her throat was totally numb and she had no idea which muscles or parts of her mouth to use to make a sound.

'I think she must be overcome with admiration. How polite.'

'There's water in the king's half of the kingdom too,' said Blossom at last breaking through.

'How do you know? It's impossible for any of my train to enter the king's half of the kingdom.'

'I haven't been there. My... I mean someone told me.'

'You're lying.'

'They shouted it out of the window.'

'I knew she'd tell us lies. Which part of her shall we hurt first?'

'The king can't go outside either because of the water.'

'Tell me why Lud fills his own territory with water,' said the queen.

'*He* isn't doing it. It's because Summer's been here too long. The apple in the water showed you that.'

'The apple in the water was obviously Lud laughing at us,' said Brigantia. 'He was saying, *You're trying to find out the spell I've used so you can undo it, but you can't and I've still got your apple.* It's as clear as the terror on your face.'

'Such a pretty face. We could start there.'

'Quiet, Mag. I want to know where she got these ideas from first,' said the queen.

'I made them up,' said Blossom quickly.

'Oh no you didn't.'

'Lies! Lies!' said Mag with glee.

Blossom felt her hands rising protectively to her face of their own accord.

'Try again.'

'I made it up.'

'More lies. This is delicious.'

As her hands rose higher and higher and the fingers separated, Blossom realised they weren't intended to cover her eyes but to hurt them.

'You are going to hurt yourself very badly,' said Mag as Blossom's index fingers, stiff and with sharp nails, began their descent towards her eyes.

'It's Jack Frost's plan. He wants Autumn to come back.'

'She's given in. Bother!'

'Jack Frost! Am I asleep not to have searched him out all these weeks? I shall enjoy scattering flakes of him in a spot where animals go to die.'

All Blossom's feelings gathered themselves in a cry that burst from her.

'Jack, get away! They know all about you.'

Her hands were still up in the air when she called out, so the patch of skin Jack had marked was only a little way from her mouth. It cooled briefly in response to her warning and then returned to its normal temperature.

The queen stood still for a few moments, concentrating hard, and then said, 'He heard you and has moved out of my reach. For the moment. You're human aren't you? You don't need to answer me. I know you are. I want to show you what happens to creatures of your kind who act out of turn.'

Light flared as Blossom was moved in an instant from the evil-darkened bedroom to another place with an uncovered window. The magic that had held her stiffly upright was taken away and her legs couldn't support her. She sank to the floor and rolled half a turn to be directly below the window and fresh air.

For a long time she lay too shocked to think. She felt as if she were a girl of snow, melting away, spreading in a pool, with not a single bone or fibre to lift her upright again. She must have slept and cried in her sleep because, when she finally began to summon her legs and fingers to her, the skin around her eyes was tight and swollen.

Her first complete thoughts as she pushed herself up onto her arms were ones of bitter regret. Why had she called on Jack to save only himself when he could have saved her too? And Caleb - she thought of him next. Why had they been so reckless as to follow Jack's instructions and, why oh why, hadn't they gone to Cornwall? If, by some impossibly good fortune, she managed to return home, she was never going to have another adventure as long as she lived. She was going to be a proper girl like Pippa and talk about nothing but clothes and giggle whenever their men teachers spoke to her.

She hauled herself above the level of the window sill and looked out. Well, she was still in the palace, and not too high up, although too high to jump, and she was almost certainly alive.

It was a while before she looked behind her into the room. The sight of grass and trees and sky, even one made by glowing stones, was very calming after her time spent staring into that disgusting cauldron. Long ribbons of gleaming grey cut across the landscape, showing how much the strange waters had taken possession of Lud's kingdom.

At last Blossom turned around to inspect the room from which she could, at that moment, see no means of escape. There was a very rough wooden bed with an unusual roll of sheets or blankets on it. Brigantia's prisoners clearly couldn't expect much in the way of comfort. It was then that the roll of bedding moved and a stick came out of it. Blossom leant as far backwards out of the window as she could. Another stick appeared and a grey lump like a ball of crinkled wool. The roll of bedding was a person.

A very, very old woman pulled herself into a sitting position on the edge of the bed and looked sadly across to Blossom. At least, it looked like an expression of sadness. Her face was such a criss-cross and zig-zag of lines, you could have constructed any expression you wanted from them.

'Come here please.'

'No. Who are you?'

Blossom was afraid that here was another goddess intent on hurting her.

'I'm Enid.'

'Enid!'

'This is how the queen punishes me. She restores me to my true age and locks me in this room with a large window so that I can see clearly how very old I look.'

She stretched out her grey stick arms and Blossom went over to comfort her with a cuddle. She had to put her twelve year-old face against what was little more than a skull lightly dressed in tissue paper and she didn't dare hug Enid hard for fear of breaking her.

'You're trembling,' said Enid.

'How does it feel to be so old?'

'I never notice my age when I look like a girl. At the moment I haven't any strength at all.'

Blossom felt that if she continued the cuddle any longer she would be ill and so she slipped her arms from around Enid and sat on the floor with her back to her. As they spoke, Enid occasionally stroked Blossom's hair. Each movement across her head was like the scraping of an old comb or the gesture of a skeleton and it made Blossom shudder.

'How long will the queen keep us here?' she asked.

'She may relent in an hour, or she may forget us. She has been known to do that. Who can tell what Brigantia will do.'

Her voice was an unrecognisable whisper and her many pauses showed that it required great effort for her to speak a long sentence.

'Do they feed you?'

'Yes, but I don't need food.'

'*I* will,' said Blossom, worried.

'What did you do to offend the queen?'

'I was looking for you and she found me near her bedroom. Kigva told her I was there. Brigantia was in her witch's shape with Epona and another even nastier old woman.'

'Mag.'

'Yes. They were making a spell. I had to own up that I was helping Jack Frost to bring back Autumn.'

'Say no more. The queen will be listening.'

'It doesn't matter if she hears that. I won't tell you any more, though.'

'Sh. She must not think there is more to tell.'

'Enid, how did you come here?'

'Curiosity caught me. Brigantia and her girls still walked in our meadows when I was your age. One evening I spied them and followed them to a staircase. I could be sleeping in our little churchyard now, in my ruff and my brocade slippers and my hands folded across my heart in peace. Instead...'

'Won't you ever die?'

'I needn't for a long, long time. Down here I age less than a year for each of the centuries that flows by above the ground.

'Can't you escape?'

'Oh yes, if I wanted to turn to dust as the first beam of real sunlight touched me. I daren't leave, Blossom, though the peace of the churchyard must be a wonderful thing.'

'I'm going to escape.'

'Don't tell me how. The walls mustn't hear.'

'I'm going to escape. Do you hear!' said Blossom very loudly to the whole of the room. She subsided again.

'Do you know how I worked out you were human, Enid? It was when you started singing. Afterwards, I suddenly thought, "It's *Sweet Phyllis Goes A-maying*." We're learning it in our music lesson at school.'

'People still sing it?'

'People of my time are always singing Elizabethan songs.'

'Am I Elizabethan?'

'Of course you are. I shall have to study Shakespeare soon, too.'

'Shakespeare?'

'Only a writer. He wrote lots of difficult plays.'

'My father said the theatre is very wicked, so I've never seen a play. Sing *Sweet Phyllis Goes A-maying* to me, Blossom. It will help me sleep.'

CHAPTER TWENTY-ONE

Three Girls

Blossom took very little notice of the tray of food that was brought. She picked up a sort of meat pasty and put it down again and did no more than splash her tongue with the juice in the jug. Having sat and stared at the tray for a long time, she forced herself to go over to the bed to see whether Enid was hungry and wanted something. Her friend seemed so fragile, so much like a loose collection of dry sticks in an old cloth bag, that she didn't dare shake her even gently in case the bag burst and what had been a friend turned into sticks scattered across the floor. She was prepared to feed Enid in the way her mother had had to break up food for granny and spoon it into her unresponsive mouth when she was so ill.

'You eat it all, Blossom. I'm better off asleep,' said Enid. 'Please don't sit so heavily on the bed.'

Blossom darted away as if Enid was radio-active. Probably even speaking too loudly could hurt her. She went over to the window and thought seriously of throwing the food tray out. She would have done so at once if she could have been sure that it would land on Brigantia's or Kigva's head. Having nothing else so do, she crumbled some of the pasty on the window sill, hoping the crumbs would attract birds. She listened. There wasn't a single note of birdsong and in the false sky of Lud's kingdom there were no arrow-shaped flocks flying home to roost. How she would have welcomed the dirtiest, most one-legged Trafalgar Square pigeon bobbing its head over her crumbs, but there the crumbs stayed, as forlorn as she was herself. It was a world which, for all its magic, couldn't conjure up the smallest evening breeze to disturb the crumbs a fraction. They could stay there for a thousand years as still as if they were carved, a piece of brilliant trickery.

So, after all, the window could offer Blossom no peace. Every part of the room was distressing. Enid on the bed could have been Enid buried for years and years, the strong door was a reminder that she was a prisoner, and all she could see from the window was a world whose stillness was never to be broken by the rustles, scampers and squeaks you heard every minute on the Heath if you concentrated. These all proclaimed: *Listen to me. I'm alive. I'm busy. Look at my new wings.*

Evening turned into night. No brilliant, soaring constellation of Cassiopeia appeared, the one that Caleb had shown her a week ago. The Blossom who had watched the dazzling splashes of The Milky Way was a younger girl entirely. If only she could come back.

Beneath the Heath, the night sky was no more than a black sheet with holes in. Blossom felt it had nothing to do with her. In fact it made her cross, as did the fact that there was no glowing gem to light the prison chamber. As night fell, the room became gloomier and gloomier. She felt more than ever the need to keep away from the bed. Enid, who might be touched or snapped by accident in the dark, was more frightening than Enid in broad daylight who could be avoided.

When it had been dark for over an hour, the door suddenly opened, startling Blossom so much by the sound it made and by the shaft of light it let in, that someone seemed to have squeezed all the skin on the back of her neck.

A girl she had never seen before stood in the doorway carrying a small leather bag. She was about fifteen, dressed all in white without jewellery, and possessed a startlingly lovely face. The gathering of cold skin at the back of Blossom's neck relaxed and she found herself smiling. Here was a girl, surely, you could trust in anything.

'My name is Dana. You have an errand to perform for the queen.'

'Of course, Dana,' replied Blossom as if the errand was to be no more than cutting a sewing thread or hunting a thimble that had rolled underneath a chair. This unknown girl was older and would protect her. She put out her right hand for Blossom to take.

'Blossom, it's Dana!' said Enid's voice from the dark corner of the room.

'It's all right, Enid. I'm being let out. I'll speak to the queen about you as soon as I can. She wants to see me. Didn't you hear?'

Dana's soft fingers applied only the lightest pressure as she drew Blossom through the doorway.

'You must meet the queen at Nemeton.'

'Nemeton! Blossom, do not...,' began Enid.

'You are very tired,' said Dana. 'You know the queen does not like you to speak too much.'

She said this very casually as if the queen's concern for her was a well-established fact.

'Nemeton. I...,' said Enid.

'Goodbye,' said Blossom. 'You'll be back to normal when we meet again.'

As she went downstairs with Dana, the few attendants they met moved away from them and bowed. Blossom enjoyed being treated with respect, but she would have liked to ask these people to explain the nervous expressions on their faces.

Dana led her out of the front door and into the night.

'I thought I had to do something for the queen,' said Blossom wondering why she wasn't being asked to do it inside the palace.

'The errand is to Nemeton.'

'Is that a place?'

Perhaps it was above the ground and near home.

'It is the queen's grove in the middle of the kingdom. All the lines of magic cross there.'

'I think Jack pointed it out to us on that first day.'

'*Us*?'

'Me.'

'You said *Us*.'

'What's this errand? It's very dark.'

Dana put her arm round Blossom's waist and pulled her close.

'You're a visitor from the upper world, aren't you? Word has got round. It doesn't matter. We're always pleased to see you. Tell me all about Jack and why you said *Us*.'

'Are we going on this errand or not?' asked Blossom.

The girl was too affectionate and too nosy and she wasn't going to let any more information slip out if she could help it. The arm round her waist squeezed her tightly and fingernails dug into her side. Blossom tried unsuccessfully to pull away.

'I'm your friend. We must hurry to the grove.'

'I'd rather not. There's water everywhere and it's so dark.'

'The queen commands it.'

'Well the queen's not here,' thought Blossom. 'You're only a girl and I'm going to get away from you.'

She tried once more to squirm free.

'The queen needs your help. We must not keep her waiting.'

'She can wait all night!'

Dana had had enough of arguing. She took hold of Blossom's wrist very securely and dragged her off into the darkness. No matter how hard she pulled in the opposite direction, and even despite her heavy fall into one of the puddles they had to wade through, Blossom couldn't release herself from the girl's grip.

What did the queen want in the middle of a wet field, in utter darkness, and a long way from the lighted palace, thought Blossom when their scrambling run finally came to an end. Dana let go of her, confident she wouldn't escape, having no obvious place of safety to run to.

'This is the middle of nowhere and you've hurt my wrist.'

'This is the heart of the kingdom. If you had obeyed instructions, I should not have needed to take you so roughly. Let us go inside. The queen is waiting.'

'Inside where?'

'Can you not see Nemeton in front of you?'

'I don't know where in front of me is.'

'Open your eyes, you foolish girl.'

Blossom squinted and shook her head. Perhaps there were some dark shapes in front of her, or perhaps there weren't. Gradually, she thought she could make out a wavy line high up where tall objects blocked out some of the glowing stones in the roof.

They had indeed reached the large clump of oak trees Jack had briefly drawn their attention to from the high palace windows. Dana led Blossom sure-footedly between the two nearest trunks, through a dense patch of undergrowth and along a narrow path that veered from side to side so that, even in daylight, the heart of the grove would have been mere leaves and darkness to anyone standing outside it.

'You have nearly passed the first circle of Nemeton. These oak trees are ages old. Stand and listen to their memories. Do you not feel the power here?'

'No, I don't,' said Blossom sullenly. 'I don't want to stand in the middle of a hedge getting all scratched. I want to speak to the queen.'

'Poor Jack Frost, thinking such a fool as you could help him. *I* am the queen. When I visit Nemeton to gain knowledge, I must come in my young girl's form. Dana is my name then. The magic power here is beyond measure. I need you to help me learn the secret of Lud's spell so that I can turn all this water against him.'

'It's not Lud doing it,' said Blossom. 'How many times do you need telling?'

'Very soon I shall open this leather bag. Follow me.'

They now passed into a grassy area containing a ring of nine pairs of tall, upright stones capped with lintels.

'First the circle of wood and now the circle of stone,' said the queen. 'The henge of Nemeton and, within it, my apple tree.'

At last Blossom could see around her, for the stones were dusted with particles of crystal that gleamed in a silvery way, lighting the circle as brightly as if there were a full moon. At the centre of the henge were Brigantia's apple tree and a kind of low, stone table which was black and didn't shine.

'I expected your apple tree to be a lot bigger,' said Blossom. 'Once I had a something tree, but nothing would it bear but a something something and a golden pear.'

'Though the presence of men is forbidden here, Lud invaded this sacred spot and stole my apple. The power should have struck him down. Now it will help me take my revenge.'

'What do you need me for?'

The queen undid the thongs which held the bag shut. She put in her hand to make sure that what she expected was still inside.

'The power will show me what use to make of you.'

'I don't like the sound of that.'

'What is there to be afraid of in a low table and a small apple tree?'

She dropped her voice for the last part of the sentence as if she were afraid of being overheard and didn't wish to give offence.

'I don't feel safe,' said Blossom.'

'I will show you.'

The queen made as if to walk between two of the upright stones but, as soon as she had broken the circle, there was a terrible rumbling and the ground began to shake. This had never happened before and she looked back at Blossom in total bewilderment. The rumbling and the shaking of the ground increased when she took another step. As she raised her foot to take the final pace that would bring her completely inside the circle, the stone pillars on either side of her lurched forwards and their heavy horizontal load slid half off. It was now poised unsteadily over the queen's head.

'Nemeton refuses me! The magic will not accept my sacrifice.'

The leather bag slipped from her hand and fell onto the ground revealing the blade of a golden dagger.

'You were going to sacrifice me!' shouted Blossom, realising now why the sight of the black stone table had been troubling her. 'I hope that stone falls on you.'

The heavy lintel scraped forwards as if pushed by her words.

'No!' cried Dana. 'Help me.'

'Use your magic.'

'I cannot use my magic here. I am only part of Nemeton. That is why I had to drag you by the arm. As Dana, I have no magic, simply a girl's strength. I dare not move. Only you can pull me free.'

'I might get crushed too.'

Very unsteadily, the queen stretched her arm backwards.

'Take my hand, child. Pull me free of the circle.'

'Why should I?'

'Please. I have no power. I cannot move.'

'Good job. Now you know what Enid feels like.'

The stones swayed as if they were as pliable as twigs.

'You've got to make some promises before I help you.'

'What are they?'

'You'll turn Enid back into a girl and never hurt her like that again.'

'Yes. Take my hand.'

'*Yes* won't do. I've got to hear you say, *I promise by Nemeton.*'

'I promise.'

'Say, *I promise by Nemeton.*'

The rage on the queen's face told Blossom how right she was to insist on this. Brigantia or Dana was not one to keep her word if she could avoid it.

'I promise by Nemeton. Pull me free.'

'That's not all. Where's the king's silver hand?'

The queen gasped at another movement of the lintel.

'It is in the darkest, deepest pool at the kingdom's end where the two streams begin. I threw it there.'

The earth shook again and the two upright stones swayed so violently you knew they were going to fall. This was Blossom's last chance to save the queen and she ran to her, took her hand and pulled her free of the circle.

When the stones tumbled, the shock was felt as far away as Hertfordshire and Essex. Mrs Belling-Peake said, 'Rupert, I do believe that was an earth tremor. Did you hear those bottles rattle?' All over Hampstead, wells that were the sources of springs feeding the Fleet River filled suddenly. Dank, mouldy draughts of air were blown out of them like popguns by the inrushing waters. Mr Belling-Peake said, 'I've heard Caleb and Blossom chattering in the junk room for the past hour. I'll go and check that the tremor hasn't worried them.'

CHAPTER TWENTY-TWO

Nemeton

As the queen lay with her face buried in the grass, pulling rhythmically at tufts of it with her outstretched hands, Blossom realised that whatever the emotion was that made Brigantia shudder and sob in this intense way, it wasn't gratitude. She caught herself wondering whether it was relief or frustration, but what a waste of precious time this speculation was. Brigantia within the grove was deprived of all her magic powers. She was only the girl Dana here.

No sooner had this thought struck Blossom than she plunged into the circle of oak trees. It was immediately dark and she knew she wasn't on a path. She could feel twigs and branches in her back, her hair, her ear. It was an unsettling feeling because, as she stood there in the dark concentrating, she knew the oak trees were deliberately obstructing her. It wasn't simply a thicket with a few branches here and there being in her path and forcing a detour; these were actively pushing her back with their fingers. A supple twig flicked across her mouth and rested lightly on her throat.

'I've got to get out of here,' she said loudly.

Immediately she felt the greenery take its hands off her and move away at least a yard. What had happened? Was she really in a little pocket of space all her own? She tried an experiment.

'Clear me a path,' she said, imitating the voice of Miss

Nanty when confronted with a corridor of girls. A path cleared.

Blossom couldn't see what had happened, but, when she moved forwards, guided only by her feet, she knew the branches had been curled back from her.

She could feel the freedom. So the grove of Nemeton obeyed the voice of young girls. When she reached the edge, she said, 'Don't let Dana out,' and jumped free.

Now she could find her bearings. She was on the same side as the distant palace and could blunder towards its lighted windows. She thought she would try giving orders in case the whole of the kingdom was in the power of young girls.

'Let me fly to exactly where Caleb is.'

She remained earthbound.

'When I walk to the palace, let me not get a wet foot.'

She got two wet feet several times over, but she arrived and was even able to slip up the staircase to the very top of the palace unseen. When she saw Caleb sitting on the top step, hunched and unhappy, she was reminded of a squirrel, its tail wrapped round it for warmth and every acorn gone.

'Thank goodness you waited for me, Caleb.'

'I didn't wait for you. I've nowhere to go.'

'Nowhere to go?'

'I haven't been down to the palace. I was frightened. I didn't want to be put in prison. And Jack's shut the passage. There's an invisible wall you can't walk through. I called and called him, but he wouldn't answer.'

'I was put in prison this afternoon, actually,' said Blossom slowly so that Caleb should get the full impact. 'It was what you read about. You know, a door you couldn't break down and they gave you your food on a tray. I didn't cry or beg for mercy or anything.' *And I didn't sit on this step all day*, she thought, but she stopped herself saying it. 'I made the queen tell me where she's hidden the silver hand. We've got to let Jack know.'

'He's used magic. I tried all day long to walk down the passage but I couldn't.'

'They know all about him. That's why he's done it. They tortured me and I had to tell them. Now he's escaped and left us here. I always said he was a bad friend.'

She gave her brother a brief account of her day and would have enjoyed the way it impressed him more if her thoughts hadn't kept returning to Enid. Like her, they were trapped down there, for the time being at least.

'We'll have to go and fetch the hand ourselves then,' concluded Caleb.

'Not at this minute, though. You don't know how dark it is out there. We could walk right into the middle of that pool by mistake.'

'If only I had the torch.'

'Brigantia might not be back yet, so we could go through her half of the palace and hide ourselves till it's light enough to see.'

Having tried once more to escape to the safety of Jack's secret room and found that his magic still blocked the way, they decided to follow Blossom's suggestion.

There were blankets in one of the store rooms. Carrying a bundle of these, they stole down through the palace. On a table in one of the corridors, they came across a tray of food and drink presumably awaiting collection. They collected it themselves and crept outside where they found the driest spot they could in a hollow far away from the palace door. Worried that their parents were worried, and frightened of what would happen if they were caught while asleep, they nevertheless ate their meal, curled up in their blankets and closed their eyes.

CHAPTER TWENTY-THREE

The Waters at the World's End

The change in the light woke them. The palace and the landscape of Lud's kingdom had half taken shape in the greyness of dawn.

'I hope they're not awake yet,' said Caleb. 'Come on. We've got to get over to the other side as fast as we can.'

Blossom reluctantly threw off her blanket and began to stroke all the stiff parts of her body.

'We haven't got time for that. Get up.'

'I ache. I got wet last night and my joints are rusty.'

'Running will loosen you up.'

'Running! Not again.'

'We can't walk there. Look how bright it's getting already.'

'Couldn't we have told the king we know where his hand is?' asked Blossom when their initial breathless run had slowed to a medium trot. She was out of puff and felt a stitch coming.

'We can't trust either of them. If Lud has the silver hand back, I bet he won't give Brigantia the apple. And if she has the hand, she'll hide it again, somewhere better. We've got to give the hand to Jack. He'll know what to do.'

'That means getting out of here. We can't get out and we can't find Jack.'

'He'll find us if we've got the hand. He's that sort.'

'We've been away all night.'

Caleb decided not to think about this and what their parents might be feeling.

They passed very wide of the grove of Nemeton, moving in dips in the ground as much as they could in case the queen hadn't yet left it.

'Fancy going on a cross country race without breakfast,' said Blossom tetchily. Her taste buds kept remembering banana milk shakes and toast and jam. 'We can't even sit down. The ground's getting sloppier and sloppier.'

'It's probably that cliff over there we want,' said Caleb. 'Can you see a waterfall?'

Water lay in the hollow roots of trees they passed and their progress was very much slowed when their leather slippers stuck in the muddy ground and came off. The streams had broadened until there were yards of water on either side of the stepping stone bridge.

'Nearly there. Nearly there,' Caleb kept saying as his sister's face became sourer and sourer. She had long given up trying to move with her dress hitched up and her sodden hem felt as if it was weighed down with stones.

'Caleb, what are those dots outside the palace! How can they be moving so fast? They're flying.'

'No, they're in chariots. And on the other side too.'

On either flank of the grove of Nemeton was a band of twenty or so people. Weapons glinted and water sprayed and now the sound of horns being blown reached them. Brigantia on the left and Lud on the right were following a V shaped course that ended where the children were.

Caleb and Blossom turned and ran as hard as they could towards the waterfall. For each of their steps, their pursuers took ten and it was soon apparent that everyone would reach the cliffs at the furthest edge of the kingdom at more or less the same time.

The cliffs were sharp and steep and there was a gleaming green algae line where one of the streams tumbled into the kingdom and made its little waterfall

The second stream descended in a deep crevice and then gushed out as if a pipe had burst. Between the two was a pool edged with square black rocks. It looked like a jaw and a set of regular teeth. The throat was the rear of the pool which disappeared into a low-arched cave at the cliff's foot.

Lud's charioteer reined in his horses. Brigantia's driver did the same.

'Ill-met!' shouted the king at his wife.

She snorted and tossed her head. Their attendants, in smaller chariots, hung back, anxious not to be tangled up in a battle of words and sorcery. The children had nowhere to retreat to because they had been caught at the very edge of the pool and the rocks that looked so much like teeth were pressing into the backs of their legs.

'It is a long time since we two have spoken,' said Lud.

'It wasn't my idea to meet you now,' said Brigantia.

'There could be peace between us and throughout our kingdom if you returned my silver hand and begged forgiveness for the grievous wrong you have done me.'

'Beg your forgiveness! I'm sure I shan't. If you give me back my apple and go on your bended knees in front of everyone and say how sorry you are for stealing it, I might begin thinking about a truce.'

'Lud bend his knee? Never.'

'That's that then.'

Raised high above the ground by the axles of their chariot wheels, they were an even more commanding pair. Whirlwinds of bitterness raged between them.

'Summer will be with us always, then.'

'Let it.'

'See how the kingdom floods through our quarrelling. The green hollows are thick with mud. The flowers rot.'

'You know what you have to do. Tell me where my apple is and then get out of that chariot and kneel down.'

Lud's laughter danced off the cliff walls. Kneel - that was a thing he could never bring himself to do.

'My Brigantia. Make me a man with two hands again and say, *I am sorry, husband.*'

'Sorry! I'm only sorry you've got one hand left. Do you see what I married, girls?'

Caleb looked at Blossom. Did Brigantia assume they wouldn't dare say where the silver hand was? Some good might come of it if Lud knew.

'We can find your hand,' he shouted and heard his own lighter voice tinkle from crag to crag in echoes.

'Tell me where, boy.'

Brigantia pointed her finger menacingly at Caleb and so Blossom said, 'We think it's in this pool behind us.'

The queen became very smug.

'These are the waters that rise from the earth's heart. Dare even the king of the gods wade in them?'

Lud looked hesitant. He was being taunted and tested in front of his bravest men.

'I can see the hand. There,' said the queen. 'A few steps and it could be yours again. Hop in if you dare.'

The waters of the pool were a greyish-yellow near the ring of stones, becoming darker towards the cave. About half way back, an object began to gleam and soon Lud's hand, giving out a strong silver light, could be seen on the pebbly bottom.

The king stepped down from his chariot and strode to the pool's edge.

'You only need to wet your boots a little,' mocked Brigantia.

Lud looked up at her, an expression of equal superiority on his face. He picked up Caleb by the back of his shirt, held him over the water for a few seconds and then let him drop. All the onlookers loudly drew in their breath.

'Why should a king do what a servant can?'

Neither Caleb nor Blossom could see any danger in the pool. The water wasn't boiling hot or poisoned as far as they could tell, nor was it over a quicksand. Once Caleb had got over the shock of sitting down in it and swallowing a couple of mouthfuls, he started to wade towards the silver hand. He moved slowly because the water was strangely resistant.

'Hurry up,' called Blossom.

'I can't. It's really hard work.'

'What's that?'

A cloud of ink was beginning to spread from the mouth of the cave through the water. Lud moved back from the edge of the pool and the horses became very restless.'

'Do hurry, Caleb.'

The inky liquid swirled around his legs and moved on to the fringe of stones. It made patterns in the water that, in the region of Caleb, held their shape. Blossom leaned over the water and screamed. They were tentacles.

As Caleb bent down to retrieve the hand, the creature's body appeared, sending a wave that splashed roughly over the black stones. People cried out and there was a frightened scrambling backwards.

'Caleb!'

The tentacles were at the front of the creature, sprouting in great numbers. Its head was very low in the water, a smooth island of glassy black, but a veined ivory beak and two round yellow eyes were clearly visible just below the waterline. As the tentacles entwined themselves around Caleb's ankles and he lifted the silver hand clear of the water, Blossom leapt into the pool. What happened then was difficult to see. The girl was splashing in her haste to reach her brother, the boy was splashing and screaming in his panic, and, before the witnesses had time to collect their thoughts or make sense of the picture, the creature had swept the children up into its infinitely armed embrace and disappeared from sight.

CHAPTER TWENTY-FOUR

Departure

They were washed through thousands of years of the history of London - past a polished axe head lying where it had first slipped from Neolithic fingers, and past the broken rim of a Roman pitcher overturned by a careless housewife too busy gossiping.

It was the course of the Fleet River they followed, the stream into which Londoners had always let their rubbish tumble and sometimes their heads. The children went through a water-filled passage that connected the dark cavern with the river as it issued from the Heath and then flowed underground to the Thames.

They were wet but not drowning, for the creature was powerful in its magic and could pass through a narrow culvert or low-vaulted tunnel in a gust of the sweetest air.

Past a butcher's knife, witness of the time when the bank of the Fleet had been a shambles and pigs for slaughter had escaped into one of its tunnels, growing fat on rubbish trapped there; through ghosts of rag and bottle where the backdoors of slums had opened to emit all manner of filth.

Now no more than a storm-drain, bricked in for all its length and driven over by people who had forgotten its existence, the little river remembered fields of cattle, wooden planks across its upper reaches and Christopher Wren's quaysides at Holborn.

Caleb and Blossom swept past all this almost insensible and burst out into the Thames beneath Blackfriars Bridge. The creature, Leviathan itself, left them on a shingle bank a little further downstream on the northern shore while it set its own course for the river mouth and the open sea. Sickened by the bickering of Lud and Brigantia, it had flooded their fields to warn them. As they refused to take notice, it now left them and the land it had secretly protected for so long. Let them fend for themselves; it was off to find a deep trench in the ocean floor where perhaps more of its kind congregated. Tired and distressed, it didn't bother to cloak itself entirely in magic while swimming away.

''Ere, did you see that bloody great lump?' said one of the workmen on the Thames Flood Barrier.

Leviathan had taken its blessing and its good luck beyond the ancient city. In farewell, it raised a curl of tentacle through the river scum that was smelling more and more of the great Atlantic expanses where it expected to make its final home.

The workman on The Flood Barrier shook his head. These polythene bags full of air, or Domestos bottles, could look like anything in the world when there was a line of them bobbing in the tide.

I'm glad we didn't get a really close look at it,' said Blossom as she and Caleb sat on the uncomfortable shingle gathering their thoughts.

A helicopter landed on a pontoon moored nearby and a man in dungarees looked over at them suspiciously.

'It didn't want to harm or frighten us. I could tell,' said Caleb. 'And it made sure I didn't lose this.'

From inside his shirt he took out Lud's hand. An arrow of silver lightning flashed up from it towards the sun and he immediately hid it again.

'We're a bit wet aren't we? People are going to stare at these costumes too. Like that man over there. What should we do?'

'Go back to the Heath I think. Today is Samhain. We must find Jack.'

'Do you know where the Heath is?'

'Not exactly. It can't be far away because that's Blackfriars Bridge.'

'Do you have any money?'

Automatically, Caleb slipped his hand into the pocket of his trousers.

'Where did these come from?'

Two ancient gold coins with designs like exploded animals lay in his palm.

'I don't remember putting them there.'

'I think the creature might have given them to you.'

'Why do you want money, anyway?'

'We ought to telephone home.'

'No. They'll make us say where we are and that'll be the end of everything. Let's find Jack first. We've got less than a day to look for the apple.'

Behind them, a rickety set of wooden steps led up to the Thames embankment.

'Which way now?' asked Blossom when they were at the top.

'Ugh! The hand moved,' said Caleb.

He took it from inside his shirt and, as before, the silver lightning sparkled upwards. Before he put the hand away again, he had time to notice that it pointed left towards the bridge.

'It knows its way home. I've got to keep it hidden, though. Do you remember Jack saying Belenos was the one who made the hand? It seems to want to keep in touch with him as well. So can we trust it?'

'I don't want to meet Belenos again,' said Blossom firmly. 'He had that rumbling voice and he was all hot.'

'You expect the sun god to be hot.'

When they reached Blackfriars Bridge, Caleb said, 'It's wriggling.'

He stood still, holding the hand through his shirt so that he could feel the way it pointed.

'This way. And let's try to keep in the shade so Belenos can't see us. He's the one who really wants Summer to stay.'

They walked along the right hand side of New Bridge Street, across Ludgate Circus and up Farringdon Street, keeping as close as possible to the shop fronts. Occasionally people raised an eyebrow at them, but all they looked like were two children whose mother dressed them eccentrically and who allowed them to play in ponds.

They had to walk by a number of sandwich bars with service counters that opened onto the street and the smell of hot sausage rolls, doughnuts and coffee was very upsetting.

'Can't we pretend we're refugees or steal something,' said Blossom. 'We could always get dad to come and pay tomorrow. Let's give them your coins, grab the food and run away.'

When they came to a greengrocer's, the hands of bananas hanging cruelly in the window had a hypnotic effect on her.

'I can't look after you *and* the hand,' said Caleb. 'Act your age.'

'I'll get that illness girls catch when they don't eat,' said Blossom. 'Mum's always warning me about it.'

'You mean she's always saying, *Don't stuff your mouth so full.*'

And so they continued, following, although they didn't know it, the course of the underground Fleet River back to Hampstead. The hand led them twisting through the cobbled alleys of Clerkenwell until at last they stood in front of King's Cross Station with its mouth-watering hamburger parlour.

'I can't go any farther,' said Blossom and Caleb knew she meant it.

As the hand appeared to be pointing towards the station, they found themselves wandering into it.

'These trains are going to Peterborough and Scotland,' said Blossom looking up at the list of departures. Jack can't expect us to go abroad.'

Caleb fingered his two coins.

'I'll try these in the Underground. If they jam the ticket machine, walk away as if we haven't done anything.'

He was given confidence by the fact that Lud's hand showed no sign of rebelling. On their way to the station, if they were about to take a wrong turning, it had clutched him.

The fare to Hampstead on the Northern Line was one pound fifty each. Caleb dropped one of his coins into the slot in the machine. He expected to hear a grinding, going-wrong sort of noise from inside and alarm bells. Instead, the ticket popped out and the coin was returned too. He put the coin back into the machine and exactly the same thing happened.

'I don't understand it. Those tiddly little coins aren't anything like modern ones,' said Blossom when they had gone through the barrier.'

'We had a bit of help. It's Platform Seven.'

On the train, they felt self-conscious, particularly when a very respectable lady got on at Camden town and glowered at them. Blossom had changed seats to be next to Caleb and left a damp patch behind her. Someone said, *Disgusting* and the very respectable lady rattled her shoulders and opened and closed her handbag to show how disgusted she personally felt.

'Leave them poor gipsy kids alone,' said a punk who was dancing to someone else's Walkman by the door. 'Look, they're holding their tickets. I can't see yours.'

'We've paid our fare, missis,' added Blossom, hoping the very respectable lady wouldn't turn up at their home for tea one day.

'Saucy minx. Hasn't your mother taught you any manners?'

'Our mother's in prison,' said Caleb. 'She cut someone's 'ead orf.'

The children giggled uncontrollably all the way through Chalk Farm and Belsize Park and then they were at Hampstead. They headed towards the corner of the Heath that touched East Heath Road north of the station. They were afraid to approach it from a point too near home in case their parents or search parties were out patrolling. Jack, they assumed, would be in a hidey-hole in the general area of Hampstead Ponds where they had met him on all the other occasions, so that meant working their way southwards again and too close to home for comfort.

As they set off across the open grass, Caleb began to wonder if all the excitement was having a peculiar effect on him. In the distance all he could see was a shimmer which soon became a blank whiteness as if he was staring into a very bright lamp. He turned his back on the light and shook his head. Blossom was doing the same.

' I can't seem to walk in that direction,' she said. 'I go blind.'

'Me too.'

'Caleb, the grass is on fire!'

Pale flames that might have been a further trick of the light danced on the tips of the grass around them.

'It's Belenos. He's trying to stop us finding Jack. Get into the shade.'

Fortunately, there was a plantation close at hand. They hurried into it and buried themselves amongst the leaves which were dark green and sappy, never being touched by direct sunlight.

The hand began flexing inside Caleb's shirt. Did it mean to lead them out into the sunlight for Belenos to trap, or did it wish to take them to Jack so he could fasten it back on Lud's arm.?

'I don't think we can trust this hand,' said Caleb. 'It looks sly to me.'

He held it away from him and watched the fingers curl up and then relax. It reminded him of a live lobster cycling slowly.

'It seems as confused as we are,' said Blossom. 'If you put it on the ground, it might point like a compass.'

'It might shoot away like a rocket.'

'Don't stand there, Caleb. There's a patch of sun.'

There were more and more of these patches of sun like golden needles cutting through the branches and piercing the air only feet from them.

'He's attacking us.'

'Look at what they do to the ground. They're red hot.'

The narrow shafts of sunlight darted down to the smell of burnt leaves and stayed solidly in the air forming a line of yellow bars. The children ran deeper into the plantation where the nettles and thorns were thickest, but where Belenos also became more confused. His shafts, which had formed at least a semi-circle around them, were now random and often a long way away.

'He *is* going to stop us reaching Jack, isn't he?' said Blossom as they crawled as far as they could under the trunk of a fallen tree. 'If he sends his sunlight exactly down here, on this very spot, it'll set all these dry branches on fire and we'll burn to death. I don't want to end up like Guy Fawkes, Caleb. I really don't.'

Immediately, and exactly together, they began running about and calling Jack's name loudly. If Jack wasn't at hand, there was no doubt that Belenos's ears were open, for the bars of hot sunlight once again found their target. As Blossom had predicted, a bundle of dead twigs began to smoulder and it was only the dampness of the rotting tree that prevented a great blaze. They ran down into a depression, a dry stream bed filled with last year's leaves. The far side of the depression was steeper and a horizontal slab of rock stuck out of it, making a shallow shelter.

'He probably can't cut through rock,' said Caleb. 'Under here quickly.'

They didn't speak as they watched the shafts from above stab the ground and then move away. Caleb nudged his sister and put his fingers to his lips. Feet were scuffing up leaves not far away. A twig snapped. Someone breathed out very noisily and there was the scraping of shoes on top of the flat stone. Blossom could feel the word *NO!* taking up the whole of her insides and struggling to burst out. The edge of their stone roof wasn't suddenly going to have a line of red-hot bars along it, trapping them in a cage, was it?

Something certainly did fall over the edge of the stone slab and onto the ground in front of them, but it was only a crumpled pair of shorts . Then there was another pair of shorts, a T shirt and a shoe.

'They're our clothes. It's Jack,' shouted Blossom and ran out from under the stone.

She turned to look at the figure who was standing higher up the bank. She hadn't been mistaken.

'Put on your own clothes and then we shall sit under the stone and talk,' said Jack.

Naturally, he didn't add, *Pleased to see you* or, *Glad you're safe.* Perhaps creatures who loved ice and snow as much as he did were simply too cold inside to show enthusiasm.

'Here's Lud's silver hand,' said Caleb proudly. 'We tracked it down for you.'

'It was not for me you did it. It was for all of us. But it is too late.'

'Can we keep the clothes?' asked Blossom.

'No. There must be no sign that you have visited our kingdom.'

Caleb clenched more tightly the two coins he had taken out of his pocket and which he hadn't mentioned. Jack didn't miss the fact that he was averting his eyes.

'Tell me,' he said sternly.

'Tell you what, Jack?' said Caleb looking down at the knot in his shoe lace.

'What you are hiding from me.'

'It's only these.' He had set his heart on keeping the coins.

'The creature gave them to him, we're sure of it, so they're not yours to take away, Jack. You keep them, Caleb and tell him where to get off. He couldn't even say *Thankyou* for the hand when all *he'd* done was run away and lock us down there. Let's go home this minute and leave him to finish his stupid adventure himself.'

She kicked her dress out of the shelter to underline her point.

'He may keep the coins. As you say, they are not mine to take. He could have found them anywhere. I *do* thank you for the silver hand. Perhaps I should have said so. It is only a pretty toy, a trinket, however. Tonight is the night of Samhain and we do not have the apple. Belenos senses that his hour has come. Smell the woodland around us. Where are the leaves splashed with red? Where are the berries of purple and black? Look — dragonflies and those black and yellow striped warriors. New buds and leaves are still appearing. The air is sweet with the lazy songs of August. All this is wrong. This is the time for the fallen apple to rot at the tree's foot, for hedgerows to be hung with Old Man's Beard. Swallows should have taken their farewell long since. Instead, they raise new broods. Where is my mist?'

'All we could get was the hand,' said Blossom.

'The king wouldn't let me near him, so how could I ask him where the apple was?' said Caleb. 'I honestly did try. I couldn't be chained up in the kitchen for ever, could I Jack?'

'So we must have the Summer always because you did not dare speak out?' said Jack looking warily over their heads and into the trees.

Caleb tearfully fingered the patterns on the coins.

'Lud kept saying that everyone was asleep, so why was I the only one who got told off? *You're all Sleepers*, he said.'

'What did Lud say about Sleepers? Tell me exactly.'

'I'll have to think a bit. He said... *I've disturbed one Sleeper. Why should I disturb another?*'

Jack put his arm around Caleb's shoulders and hugged him tight. It was a gesture of delight that left the children speechless. It would also have left Caleb very cold if Jack's power hadn't been so weak. They could see nothing of any importance in the remarks Caleb had repeated. He might just as well have come out with, *Ya boo, wobbly poo,* for all the significance the words seemed to have.

'The Sleeper. The Sleeper. Yes, the Sleeper,' said Jack to himself.

'Tell us what it means, Jack.'

'It means the apple. I, Jack, have found its hiding place. Neither you nor Lud knew what he had told you.'

'Go and get it now and pinch it and we can all go home,' said Blossom.

How could he have the cheek to say, *I, Jack, have found its hiding place* when he'd sneaked off and Caleb had to risk being chained up?

'It is not in my power to disturb a Sleeper. You were right when you said you thought the apple was in a place that was forbidden to my kind. The Old Magic will not let me pass, but to you, I feel, the magic will be a curtain and not a wall. You are young and human, the things I am not. You may draw the curtain and take the apple. How my fingers itch to pinch it.'

'Who is this Sleeper?'

'Ah. I must take care and tell you what you need to know and no more. Before we came to these islands, and that was long enough ago, there were other powers here who protected the people of stone and bronze. Rather than share the land with us, they chose to be buried and sleep until such time as - I do not know. What will awaken them is their secret, not ours. There is a Sleeper in a mound on your Heath.'

'That's the mound they call *Boadicea's Grave*.'

'Do they? She would be pleased to know that. Though you might dig a shaft through the mound or flatten it and in its place grow corn, you could not displace the Sleeper. They are here and there in places I shall not tell you. So, Lud hurled Brigantia's apple into the heart of that mound, into the Sleeper's hand. Even he must leave it there. You are another matter.'

'When do we go and get it back?'

'By night. If we walked towards the Sleeper now, a ring of fire would encircle his mound and I, Jack Frost, the prince of cold, would shrivel in it.'

'You mean we've got to come onto the Heath at night again?' asked Blossom. '*You* don't have any parents, Jack, but it's not fair to mum and dad for us to be out two nights running with them not knowing where we are.'

'They know where you are. That is to say, they think they know where you are. I have spoken to them.'

'Have you told them the truth?'

'I have told them what they needed to know. That is truth enough. I made my voice like your friend Marion's. She said she wanted your company and that you would eat and sleep with her.'

'I hope you didn't use exactly those words, Jack. That isn't how Marion talks. She says, *Oh my little darling, come and kiss your poor old Marion.*'

'I did not use those words either,' said Jack, 'but I used good words.'

The children smiled at his insistence that he had acted his part convincingly.

'It's funny how you can always drum up a little more magic when you need it,' said Blossom. 'You said you were dying not so very long ago.'

She couldn't forgive the way he had shut his hiding place against them. Whatever the danger, she felt, you shouldn't trample on your friends.

Even Jack managed a half wink.

'You read me well, little one. My skin is too pale to blush, but I blush inwardly. To encourage you, I perhaps made death seem a little nearer, but, be certain, if we do not find the apple by Samhain midnight, an old old man will be found dead tomorrow where we stand now.'

'We haven't failed yet,' said Caleb.

'Nor shall we,' said Jack. 'Let Belenos sport with his flames this afternoon. Soon he shall see a true Samhain fire that burns all the growth of Summer and prepares the way for Winter. Once, on Samhain Eve, bonfires blazed throughout the land and men and beasts passed through their smoke for good luck.'

'We'll do that for good luck on Bonfire Night,' said Blossom. 'It's only a week away.'

'For the moment you must return home and rest. I shall sit here and release what magic I can from this fidgety hand. Remember, Lud uses it to summon Autumn storm clouds and though, without the apple, it is not strong, I think I can manage a speck or two in Belenos's eye. A few small clouds I mean. One will cover your way home so that he does not harm you. Be gone now and follow the streets. It will be safer.'

They walked away trusting that there was a cloud above them to ward off the golden darts. When they had climbed out of the stream bed and started to pass amongst the trees, Blossom looked back. Jack was crouching in the space under the stone which moved slowly down in front of him like a garage door.

'Don't look so excited about meeting the Sleeper,' she snapped at Caleb. 'You know it's certain to be extremely dangerous.'

CHAPTER TWENTY-FIVE

The Sleeper

'You're home soon,' said Mrs Belling-Peake. 'It didn't take you long to get tired of Marion. She doesn't order bananas by the ton. Is that it?'

'We've only come home for a rest and then we're going back.'

'There's no point if she's coming to the party.'

'What party?'

'My last minute Hallowe'en party. She should have told you. I thought she sounded a bit vague on the telephone yesterday. Don't tell her I asked you this, but has she been - you know what?'

'Drinking?'

As the children had been surviving by their wits for the past few days, it was an easy matter for them to discover what had happened in their absence. They learnt that, despite the earth tremor, the planned visit to Cornwall had been abandoned because they were so opposed to it that they were willing to sleep at Marion's. Now, if the family were going to have to stay in smelly old Hampstead, and it was Hallowe'en, why not have a party?

'Funny Mr Frost has rung up again,' said Mrs Belling-Peake. 'He said he was sorry he couldn't keep his last appointment with dad because he was having trouble with his apple trees but he's free tomorrow. At least, that's what I understood him to say. When I invited him to the party, he said dressing up as witches and warlocks was ridiculous. Dad thinks he's an eccentric genius and that we should humour him.'

While their parents were out shopping for the party, Caleb telephoned Marion.

'Marion, this is Caleb.'

'Caleb who?'

'The only Caleb you know. Aldona's little Caleb.'

The words filled his mouth with pins.

'*My* little Caleb too. Why don't you ever come and see me?'

'You've got to tell mum and dad we stayed with you last night because we didn't want to go to Cornwall.'

'Did you stay with me?'

'No, but we want you to tell them we did or we'll be in terrible trouble.'

'How many days have you been staying with me? I didn't notice you. You should have waved or something.'

'We didn't stay with you. We just want you to say we did.'

'Was it two days or three?'

'All right. It was two days and I'm ringing to say thank you very much but we won't be coming back.'

'What a shame. Shall I bring your things over?'

'We brought them with us.'

'Good.'

Then he told her about the party which she understood better.

The children were fast asleep, fully clothed, on top of their beds when their parents returned. They didn't stir as they were undressed, had their faces sponged and were slid under their duvets.

'They look exhausted,' said Mr Belling-Peake.

'I thought we might let them stay up late. They're almost old enough not to be precocious and get under everyone's feet. Won't there be tantrums tomorrow if they miss the party?'

Mrs Belling-Peake wrote a note to each of them which said, *If you wake up while the party's still going on, come down and say hello to the guests.*

Mr Belling-Peake added firmly underneath, *But not if it's after ten-thirty.*

Caleb woke first, looked at his watch, saw it was nine o'clock and yelped.

Blossom was still deeply asleep, muttering to herself and scratching the cold spot on her hand. Its summons couldn't penetrate beneath the many layers of her tiredness. Caleb, with his hand on her shoulders and swinging her violently from side to side, could do the job much better.

'We've only got three hours, Blossom. It's night-time already.'

Blossom was warm and heavy. She had to struggle very hard to push back her bedclothes.

'It's just like the first time,' said Caleb a little later. 'Here we are creeping down the stairs while they're having a party.'

Blossom's withering look needed no words to reinforce it.

This time they couldn't avoid the adults. Mrs Belling-Peake appeared from the sitting room at the very moment they stepped onto the bottom stair and swept them into the heart of the fun. Marion sat by the french windows wearing a slightly bent witch's hat and staring into an empty glass.

'I'm going to dilute this punch for you children,' said their mother. 'Now you can circulate, but don't try and be too clever. It gives adults the pip.'

'If only they knew,' Blossom whispered as she and Caleb looked at the various witch and warlock costumes sported by the guests. A *real* witch was waiting on the Heath to stop them handing her apple to Jack. They promised themselves ten minutes and then they would escape.

'Marion hardly seems to remember that the children stayed with her last night,' Mrs Belling-Peake said to her husband. 'I expect she forgot to feed them and that's why they came home. They were too loyal to say what a state she was in. Wasn't it thoughtful of Caleb to ring her with a reminder about the party?'

Just when Caleb thought he saw a good moment for slipping away, one of the male guests decided to play the *Guess who I am* game with the children. He was one of those wearing a full face mask, hook-nose, warts, devil's horns, and they hadn't the slightest idea who he was. They were desperate to guess his identity and send him on his way and the more frantic they became when they failed, the greater joke he thought it was.

'Isn't it an oppressive evening?' said Mrs Belling-Peake. 'I don't mean the famous Hampstead pong which my joss sticks are bravely battling with. There's a sort of odd atmosphere. If we had a dog, I'm sure it would be affected. Good Heavens! Was that another earth tremor or a heavy lorry going by?'

'It was a gin and tonic,' said Marion. 'Thank you.'

'Here you are,' said Mrs Belling-Peake filling Marion's glass with lemonade and assuming she wouldn't notice what she was being given. Marion poured the drink straight onto the floor without looking at it. Before the poor hostess had time to make her feelings known, a late guest appeared at the french windows.

'Mr Frost. So you decided to come after all. How nice. Where are your long nose and your warts?'

'We'll look after him, mum.'

'Thank you, darling. Take him over to the food, not out into the garden.'

Impatient, trembling, relieved, they poured any old drink into a glass for Jack and grabbed someone's half-eaten plate of food so they could get out of the house as quickly as possible.

'Not like that, Blossom. I'm sure Mr Frost doesn't want leftovers.'

'Mum, don't interfere. Anyway, I think Marion's going to start singing.'

'Excuse me a moment,' said Mrs Belling-Peake and Jack was able to slip an arm round each of the children and have them outside in a twink.

'I have waited for you.'

'We fell asleep and then we had to come to the party.'

Soon, all three were in the street.

'Walk slowly and gather yourselves,' said Jack. 'This will be my night or theirs. Who can tell where they are lying in wait for us or what they mean to do.'

Blossom had been about to squeeze his hand and say, 'It's going to be all right,' as her mother did when they sat in the dentist's waiting room. Now she wasn't so confident.

'Have you got the silver hand with you, Jack?'

'Never worry about that. Jack knows many a secret hiding place for silver hands.'

When they reached the edge of the Heath, Jack recoiled with a faint cry. The children drew back too, their faces brushed by a strange heat.

'What is it, Jack?'

'They have covered the Heath in a shroud of fire. Though I do not like it, I can walk through it and so can you.'

The air was clinging and heavy, yet not damp, like dry treacle. Above their heads, the stars were immediately put out by the fuzzy heat haze.

'It's sort of red,' said Blossom and it's hurting me to breathe.'

'This is a mockery of defence, as if one should build a castle wall of leaves,' said Jack. 'There will be worse than this. Forward.'

'It's not that far to the mound,' said Caleb taking heart from the fact that they were making steady progress.

'Cernunnos!'

'That is Lud himself. He is above the ground. Keep on.'

'Cernunnos! You, Jack Frost.'

'I'd know *her* voice anywhere,' said Blossom.

'Cernunnos! Our rivalry comes to a head.'

'That is Belenos. He has waited so long to singe my wings.'

Out of the darkness, three groups of figures moved towards them.

'They come at us from all sides, yet they are not together. In their division must lie our safety,' Jack whispered to the children.

'Talk properly!' Blossom shouted.

'I mean, set one against the other. I mean...I mean...'

When his own life and the last Autumn of all on Earth were threatened, he could only speak his own language. Why wouldn't these difficult children understand? But they had been chosen.

'I shall make the flames crackle between your toes and then up your long shanks to your icy heart,' said Belenos. 'There are many thousand years of old scores to settle.'

The children cowered behind Jack and he let them wring his slender fingers.

'Do something!'

'Use your magic!'

'The Sleeper will not let you or that child take the apple from his mound,' said the deep voice of Lud. 'We have found an ancient magic guarding it tonight. Your efforts are wasted and I shall leave you to Belenos's mercy unless you give me back my hand, which I know you have.'

'No apple, no hand,' said Jack

'Well, someone's got to break the Sleeper's ring of enchantment. I want my apple, but Jack Frost's not going to pinch it,' added Brigantia shrilly.

She put her hand on her hip and squared up to her husband. He took a deep breath and, from his four inches of greater height, looked down into her fierce eyes.

'I say no-one shall try to disturb the Sleeper unless my hand is returned.'

'And I say I'm going to have my apple back and no-one else is going to lay a finger on it.'

Lud made a vague gesture with his hand. Frankly he didn't care who had the apple or what they did with it. All he wanted was to sit by a dying fire resting his head in both hands and be melancholy while the blind harper plucked on the strings of his heart. Now here was Belenos saying, *You've got to act this way and show who's king*, and Brigantia antagonising him into acting exactly the opposite way from what she wanted, as usual.

'Have you gone to sleep standing up, like a horse?'

As Lud's thoughts clouded his eyes, Brigantia had moved to within a foot of him. He shook his head and couldn't at once summon the energy to return her stare.

'Why are we always like this?' he asked her softly.

'Give me my apple and we won't be,' she replied, determined that *he* was the one who was going to give in.

'One more time, Cernunnos. Where is my silver hand?'

'Though you turn me to steam, I shall never tell you unless the Autumn comes.'

Taking the children by surprise, Jack swung them away from him. He had felt the flames of Belenos's impatience start under and between his toes as promised.

'Remember you have been chosen,' he said as the first twinges of pain hit him.

Caleb had stumbled and fallen and, as he picked himself up, he looked back and saw Jack's predicament.

'Tell him where the hand is!'

'Go,' said Jack. 'Do not join me in the circle of flame.'

Caleb stared mesmerised until Blossom took his hand and jerked him away. They attempted to dodge Brigantia who spun round and pointed a menacing finger at them. Before a bolt of magic had time to shoot from those hard fingernails, Blossom called at the top of her voice, 'I saved you in Nemeton and you can't touch us.'

'No, I can't. I can't! I can't!'

The queen's frozen look of superiority broke up into wrinkles of temper. She stamped her foot and the king laughed.

'Run from her as fast as you like,' he growled. 'You will never disturb the Sleeper.'

He motioned for Belenos to stay his ground as Caleb and Blossom were lost in the darkness. He laughed again but this sound and Brigantia's mutterings of frustration were covered by other sounds - the thud of their feet, the roaring of their breath and Blossom saying again and again, 'We'll find the mound because we want to.'

They did find it, or at least Caleb on his own saw the tree-covered tumulus and its protective railings emerge from the darkness, because Blossom had been overtaken by a stitch and was lying exhausted further back on the grass. Lud and Brigantia were there also, barring his way. They could fly from spot to spot and didn't have to huff and puff through the night like the eleven year old boy whose face fell when he saw them.

'Yes, I am waiting here to punish you,' said Lud. 'There will be no escape. Those who act against me are always punished as your friend Jack is being punished now.'

He gave a sideways glance at his wife who had tried desperately to approach the mound, but the old spell held firm.

Caleb imagined his fate. Was he to be dragged down a rabbit hole into Lud's kingdom? The cook was probably boiling the oil ready to pour over him in revenge. Hot tears splashed off the top of his cheeks and seemed to reach as far back as his ears.

The king let his words sink in. There was plenty of time to gather up this meddlesome child in a swirl of magic and plant him in a dungeon. Brigantia might be prohibited from touching him, but she would see that Lud himself enforced the law severely.

Was the boy going to throw himself at his feet? It would do no good. Sobbing, Caleb hurtled forwards and grasped the railings behind the king. Some instinct said hold on to them and never let go. He turned round to face Lud, making sure with each part of the movement that he always had at least one set of fingers firmly clasping an iron upright.

Lud came no nearer. Caleb shook his tears away, he didn't dare release his hands to wipe them, and gave a little smile. Lud began to look uneasy and Brigantia was visibly relaxing.

'You've miscalculated, O Great King,' she said. 'The boy's inside the enchanted circle and you're outside. Go on, brat, climb over the fence. He can't touch you. Just remember who that apple belongs to.'

'The Sleeper keeps me out and lets him in,' said Lud.

'That's right. The Sleeper obviously believes in giving apples back to their true owners.'

The railings were very high for a boy of Caleb's size. There was no lower bar he could use as a foothold. He had to put his hands on the horizontal top and hitch himself up until he could rest his knees there and then, springing over the sharp points, drop onto the other side. Even then he had time to think, 'They're gods and they're watching me.' A hundred yards away across the Heath, he saw a glow and thought in a panic, 'That's Jack burning.'

Blossom had recovered enough to drag herself to the mound. She stood behind the group of onlookers and, like them, fixed her eyes on her brother. He scrabbled on the ground for a while and then suddenly threw his head back as a kitten does when you take it by the scruff of the neck. Silver spangles appeared all over him and he slowly sank into the ground.

Blossom screamed and launched herself at Brigantia, intending to punch her as hard as she could. Her attack bounced off the magic surrounding the queen.

'If my brother doesn't come back safely, I'll tell that thing with the tentacles to get you,' she said.

'I don't know what you're talking about.'

'Yes you do. It might have looked like a monster, but it was on *our* side. And no-one's tried to drop a rock on *my* head.'

'*I'd* love to drop a rock on your head.'

'You can't hurt me because I saved you.'

'And *you* can't hurt *me*. Bc quiet, you stupid girl. The Sleeper has taken your brother in. I don't expect he'll hurt him.'

'He better not.'

Blossom began to think where she could get an excavator in the middle of the night to dismantle the mound if Caleb didn't appear soon. In the end, her agitation got the better of her and she barged between the king and queen and stood shaking the railings. No-one was able to touch her there and so she was able to shout, 'Caleb, come back!' until she was hoarse.

There was a long period of silence and then Lud called, 'See now.'

The spangles had reappeared on top of the mound like a weak fountain. The fountain bubbled higher and Blossom saw Caleb rise up enveloped in silver that might have been the shell of another body outside his own.

'The sleeper has released him.'

Caleb turned and looked at them. An arm was raised, but it was an arm made of silver, not one of Caleb's arms, both of which hung limply at his sides. A silver finger pointed accusingly at Lud, Brigantia and Belenos in turn and then the shape of a silver body slid down into the earth leaving Caleb behind.

Blossom called her brother's name at least six times before he was aware of her. He focused on them all and then raised a small apple high in his right hand.

'Give it to me at once,' shouted Brigantia.

Lud gave the same order.

Caleb turned the apple slightly in his hand as if he couldn't believe it was at last nestling in his fingers.

'You heard me,' called Brigantia, but, almost before the words had reached his ears, the apple was soaring over her head in the direction of the distant glow that was brighter now and a better target.

Blossom held her breath. Brigantia had reached up for the apple as if to pluck it from the sky. She needn't have worried. A power stronger than Caleb's skinny arms lifted the apple and sped it on its way.

They knew immediately that Jack had caught it and pinched a wrinkled scab in its polished skin. The heat disappeared like a lifted curtain and the stars were suddenly frostily clear. There was a flurry of dead leaves, one of which settled on Brigantia's shoulder. She picked it off and crumbled it into little pieces.

'He's won,' she said. 'We've got to put up with him for another Autumn and Winter.'

'No-one has won or lost,' said Lud. 'It is as it should be. The world has moved on in its course and the year has turned. This is good.'

'I'm not totally sure it's good,' said Brigantia. 'I was really enjoying Summer. But at least we've nothing left to quarrel about.'

Then Jack was among them. His face was as thin as ever, but its pointedness was now a sign of strength. His clothes had almost no shape. They shifted in patterns like snow drifts in a wind. He stood in front of each of the most important of them, the gods of streams and stones and wooded, shady places, the whole Pantheon of ancient spirits Mr Belling-Peake would have called it, and each had to bow his or her head to acknowledge that they had entered Jack's season.

'You may bow your head lower than the rest,' he said to the tanned and golden-curled Belenos.

'I bow and you know I would burn you if I could.'

'Summer and Winter. We are opposites and must always contend. It is the scheme of things. So you tried to burn me

176

with your Summer fire, did you? It reached my shins. Tonight is Samhain and before this night is done, there will be such Samhain fires, such riven trees, such flashes in the sky as you have rarely seen.'

'May a king ask for his silver hand after all this?'

'He may and soon it will be returned to him.'

Finally it was the children's turn.

'Behold the Lord of Autumn gales. Do you not tremble to be near him?'

'No. You'll always be Jack to us and we're not bowing. Magic us home, please, before you forget Caleb found the apple for you. Look at him. He's tired out.'

CHAPTER TWENTY-SIX

Conclusion

The children shared the same troubled and noisy dreams. It wasn't so much what they saw as what they sensed that made their dreams disturbing. They were aware of haste and panic and the rapid beating, beating, beating of small creatures against the storm winds, lighthouses, windows.

During the course of the night, the flap in the back door swung in as a ginger cat, wet and terrified, decided that Blossom's bed was a safer place than a flashing, dripping garden.

Mrs Belling-Peake lay with long trails of cotton wool out from her ears and across the pillow, and still she jerked with each crash of thunder. She was half afraid it was, in actual fact, a succession of earth tremors building up to one cataclysmic bang when the house and the whole world would disintegrate around her.

In the morning when she woke, Blossom knew that things were different. It wasn't simply that Percy was curled up and purring in the crook of her knees, a spot he had rejected for months; there was something totally different about the light itself. With a frown on her face, she moved the cat down the bed and got up. She found herself shivering and searching for the warm slippers she had pushed under the chest of drawers.

When she drew the curtain back, she saw at once why the bedroom was lit with a new, pearly light. The window was covered with intricate patterns drawn in frost. She had no doubt Jack had done it with his own fingers, transformed overnight into icicles. She would have liked, *Thank you , Blossom, you were wonderful* , etched in large letters like the message on a birthday cake, but she had to be content with scrolls and interweaving curls that reminded her of the patterns on the brooch she had worn in the country below the Heath.

They had managed it in the end - Autumn had come, and two red and yellow leaves frozen to the window sill underlined the point.

She went into Caleb's room to share the news with him and found him sitting up in bed reading, his pillows stuffed behind his back and his tartan rug round his shoulders.

'I've been looking up my coins,' he said. 'They're gold staters of the first century BC. The designs are a horse made of lines with a chariot wheel underneath its middle, a giant ear of corn and lots of other lines the book says are a god and goddess, but I can't see it. They don't have a king's name on so you can't be sure which king minted them.'

Blossom ran the tip of her finger over the horse and gave her brother a conspiratorial look.

'We don't need to tell mum and dad about them. They're our proof. As long as *we* know, that's all that matters.'

At breakfast, Mrs Belling-Peake was very jittery.

'Don't go into the garden yet, darling,' she said to Blossom. 'It's sprinkled with dead birds. The swallows have gone all of a sudden, but the storm was too much for some of them. And my poor apricot tree. If I didn't know it was the wind and rain, I'd swear someone had deliberately wrenched it off the wall and snapped every single branch. You can't imagine what a shock I had when I opened the back door and saw the chaos.'

Mr Belling-Peake had gone into the cellar before breakfast to check that the previous night's rain hadn't flooded it. He emerged when the family were finishing their meal.

'Rupert, why are you carrying that lump of concrete?' asked Mrs Belling-Peake.

'It isn't concrete, it's part of the cellar floor. I moved it yesterday to look at the damp underneath. This morning I turned it over and what did I find?'

He made a sound like a trumpet fanfare and spun the block of stone so that the other side was visible.

'Oh, it's a carving.'

'If I'm not mistaken, it's pre-Roman.'

He put the stone carefully on the table.

'I'm so excited. It's weathered and unclear, but I think it's the Celtic mother goddess in her three forms.'

'Dana, Brigantia and old warty,' Blossom could have told him.

So Jack knew how to say thank you after all.